I0695013

The Divine Do-over

A novel by Sana' Watts

ISBN-13: 978-1-965352-94-6

Dedication:

To all the vocational missionaries, may you feel seen and represented - even a little bit. To all those who struggle with shame, may you know the God who clothes you. To all my fellow people-pleasers, or even parent-pleasers, may you grow in courage to please God alone.

SANA' WATTS

Acknowledgements

I have to thank Power to Change Students for allowing me to use parts of their trainings that they go through with their missionaries. In this book, and in my life, you have been an invaluable resource.

I must also thank Rebecca and Fred-Eric for being my Haitian ambassadors, giving me insight into the culture. I hope I represented Haitian culture well.

Next, I must thank Kayne. You were a huge inspiration for Josué, with his testimony, tattoos, and compassionate pushback on the North American church. Thank you for being a pseudo-muse. You are dearly loved.

Cynthia, thank you for this gorgeous cover! Diane, thank you for your feedback on this manuscript. You make me a better writer, to the glory of God.

Des, Josué is also inspired by you. I love your love for missionary work and missional living. I love your passion for loving international students. I love you - period. It is my honour to be your helpmate.

And to Yahweh, "to Him who loves us and has freed us from our sins by his blood and made us a kingdom, priests to His God and Father, to him be glory and dominion forever and ever. Amen."

Chapter 1

I am a nobody. I am average. I am unnoticed. I am Gaelle Louissaint.

I am the person who gets bumped in the school hallway because no one realizes that I'm there. The one whose name is easily forgotten upon an introduction.

I hate that this is who I am now.

But now it's familiar to me; a tolerable hate. One where I don't like my life right now, but I'm used to it - and changing it would be so much more difficult than just continuing on.

Plus, it's not like I'm like this all the time. I have my hangouts with Ruthia on the weekend and at least I'm still modelling.

It's only at school where I'm a living blob of nothing. Speaking of, or rather thinking of, I should stop ruminating and get ready. I barely glance at myself in the mirror as I get ready, familiar with my cinnamon brown skin, big dark brown eyes, and symmetrical features. What used to take me a good hour back home now takes all of five minutes. Pull on track pants and a hoodie, pull my faux locs into a ponytail.

Done.

For the umpteenth time, I wish we hadn't moved. I wish I was still in my beloved Montreal. The old architecture, the city vibes, Mount Royal, readily available poutine - I miss it all.

More than the place, I miss who I was when I was there; comfortable and confident. What I feel in snippets here was a 24/7 reality. It's that sense of home that I'm missing, I guess. That knowing that you belong, and you're safe. I didn't even feel this … lost when my papa dropped out of the picture. I shake my head, trying to pre-emptively get rid of the memories, to no avail. I can still remember it like it was yesterday, although it was nine years ago.

~

It's Early Release Day and I'm so excited. Manman took a half day from work to pick me up from school so that we can spend the afternoon together watching movies. We reach home and I hear a sigh. And then a giggle.

I drop my backpack and tiptoe towards the sound. Manman is quiet beside me as I go up the stairs; making sure that I don't creak them as I follow the sounds.

More sighs. A few gasps. A few giggles. And a few moans. I don't know what those sounds mean, but they must be bad because Manman looks like she wants to throw up.

And then we reach the source of the sound; my parents' bedroom. And the door is wide open.

I see my dad with no clothes on.

I see a blond lady, covered by tangled sheets

My whole body tensed. I don't know what is going

on. Or who this lady is. But I am sure that none of this can result in something good.

And then I look beside me at Manman.

She looks like she might cry. Or faint. Or scream. She looks so hurt.

I'll never forget that face.

Papa is frozen; he watches my mother, seeing what she will do. The lady is doing the same. And then, quietly, almost so quiet that I don't hear her, she says, "Sortez [get out]."

When he doesn't move, her voice rises. "Get. Out." he moves, putting on clothes and the lady does the same.

"Je n'ai pas dit: 'habillez-vous et, puis, sortez, s'il te plaît.' J'ai dit: Sortez!" [I did not say, get dressed and then please leave. I said, Get Out!] my mother yells, her voice shrill, her eyes full of rage.

And that's when my papa ran. The last thing I saw was his boxers and a trail of blond hair.

Once they are gone, the tears come. And come. And come.

Watching your manman cry is a horrible experience. She seems to be unable to enter their room and sits on the floor instead, leaning against the hallway wall.

I sit beside her and wrap my arms around her. My eyes fill with tears to see my manman in so much pain.

But they fall for me.

Even though I'm not sure what happened, I know that something horrible has happened to our family. Some part of me knows he was supposed to stay. He was supposed to say sorry. He was supposed to fight for our family.

Instead, he ran away. I feel a pain in my chest as I take in his abandonment.

How is it possible to miss someone who has hurt you? That shouldn't be possible. It's so unfair.

~

I wipe away a few tears as the memory fades from my mind. I hate that his betrayal still can affect me so much. He deserves none of me, not even my sad feelings. I missed him then, but I don't anymore. Especially not with Don in our lives. I smile as the memory of meeting him comes back to me.

~

It's a Wednesday and we are shopping for pads when we see a guy in the same aisle. I feel my cheeks warm. It's my first time buying them and I am embarrassed enough without having some random guy looking at the things I am going to use every 28 days.

He is about 6 feet with dark red hair, bordering on auburn, soft green eyes, and a few freckles. He trips over his feet when he sees us, probably because my manman is a babe.

After he recovers from tripping, he approaches us. "Hey, I know that this may seem forward, but would you like to go out Saturday night?"

"You're right, that is forward. Especially since you're married." My manman's voice is cold as she gestures to a silver ring on his left hand.

"What? I'm not- I'm not married."

"Is that not a ring on your finger?" This struck too close to home for her.

"This is my graduation ring!" He says back and then takes it off so that we can read the inscription. Class of 1987.

"*Right, and I'm supposed to assume you're just buying pads for your sister?*"

"*Yes!*"

My manman harrumphs.

He sighs. "*Look, here's the text she sent me asking to buy them for her.*"

He takes a cell phone out of his pocket and taps the screen a few times. Then he holds it out to us. We lean in forward to see the message: '*Hey bro! Can you pick me up a pack of pads? I'll pay you back later with some steak! Lol. Thx! :)* '

"*Oh.*"

"*Yeah, oh. It is apparent that I'm not married and am picking up pads for my sister.*" *There is a bit of an edge to his voice.*

"*I'm sorry... sir. It's just that I've been in a relationship where there was infidelity and I didn't want to see it happen to anyone else.*" *She turns to me.* "*Gaelle, let's hit another store instead for what you need, okay?*"

I nod in agreement. We turn around and walk away.

"*Wait.*"

My manman and I pause and turn back around. "*Yes?*"

"*I respect you for inquiring if I was married. And I understand about what you went through. My fiancée cheated on me a week before our wedding. That's why I guess I was so offended, because I could never hurt someone else that way. But I'd still like to go out with you Saturday, or earlier if you're free.*"

"*You'd still ask me out after I was being so rude to you?*" *She is clearly surprised.*

"Yes. We have more in common than just being easy on the eyes," he winks.

My manman giggles. Oh my gosh, who is she even?

"I'm free tonight. By the way, my name is Béatrice Louissaint, and this is my daughter, Gaelle."

"My name is Don. Don Frances."

I can't help but smile at the memory, even though meeting Don upended our lives. It was amazing how much he lavished love on my mother. And he didn't try hard to be my father. He was almost more like an uncle to me. I just wish that his work hadn't transferred him to Toronto. And that they had talked with me first before deciding to move. I know my manman loves me, but sometimes it feels like they have a new life together that doesn't really include me; like they are tolerating me until I go off to university.

The thought of that just saps the life out of me, leaving this blah in my place. If it weren't for Ruthia's friendship and still continuing to model, I would probably kill myself. What else would there be to live for?

I sigh again and then check the time on my watch. Yikes, I'm late. Which means I'll have to skip breakfast, not that I'm super hungry, anyway. Besides, it keeps me skinny for the job.

Don and Manman are already gone, which spares me from experiencing their guilt and pity. At least I'm capable of being thankful that school is only a fifteen-minute walk away from where we live; ten if I speed walk.

I hear the school bell go off as I walk in the doors. Since no one around me is rushing, it must be the warning bell. I keep my head down as I walk over to my locker. Once I'm there, I unpack my bag and grab the books I need for class. As I close my locker, I see *him* walking down the hallway.

Josué Désulmé.

The tallest 12th grader in the school, broad shouldered, with deep brown skin, light brown eyes and his hair in twists - he is the most handsome guy in school to me. No contest. It didn't hurt that we're both Haitian, well - he's half, but still. My heart flutters as he passes by me, and I use my willpower to hold in a lovesick sigh.

Yeah, my capacity to have a crush didn't change when I moved.

The difference is, back home, I would've been vibrant enough to catch his attention. I would've been confident enough to talk to him.

Not now.

Plus, I'm not the only one who likes him. I've overheard girls in my gym class talking to each other about the guys that they like. The thing is, they don't like him for the right reasons.

Yes, he's hot. There's no denying that. But he's also super-talented - his artistic skills are off the charts. And he's kind. When I first got here and was a little lost, he helped me figure out how to get to my class. I didn't understand why he would deign to talk to me, but he did.

And there began an unrequited crush.

Which I can live with. I mean, I have been living with it, and it has to go away. Crushes don't last forever, after all.

Right?

The second bell rings and jolts me out of my thoughts. Great, now I'm late for my first class.

What a wonderful way to start my day.

Chapter 2

This Tuesday was unlike any other. For the first time since we moved here, I've had a photoshoot on the morning of a school day.

My mom normally refuses those jobs for me, since she says that school is my priority. This one, though, paid way too well to decline.

It was a fun time. I was in the role of a younger sister to an older model, and we were showing how the product fit multiple generations. She was a stunning Black woman whose hair was loc'ed. I rarely get to see other Black models, much less with hair so unconventional. To think that this often superficial and shallow world made space for someone like her. It was just, wow. Although she was gorgeous so that helped matters.

Still, she was inspiring to me.

When I get to school, I had only missed my first two classes. I go straight to my locker but can feel eyes on me. What is going on? Is there toilet paper on the bottom of my shoe? Something on my face?

I move my hand to my face and then remember that I'm wearing makeup. I was in such a hurry to get here on time that I didn't clean my face before arriving.

Added to that, I am not sporting my typical sweats, hoodie, and ponytail. Instead, I am wearing leggings with a long sleeve crop top and my hair is in the same updo that was arranged on the shoot. I guess I look different from how people see me at school.

This is what I usually looked like back home.

It doesn't matter, though. Tomorrow, I'll be invisible again. They won't remember me.

I hum to myself as I do my combination and then see a shadow fall on my locker. I turn around to see Josué inches away from me.

"Your name's Gaelle, right?"

I nearly faint. He knows my name? I try not to let my mouth open in shock and then clear my throat, knowing that otherwise my voice would squeak. I decide to play it casual.

"Yeah, and you're Josué?" As if I don't already know.

"Yeah, I was wondering I'd you'd want to hang out with me right now. Since it's lunch and all. We could hit the mall and get something to eat?"

Oh, my goodness. He was asking me out.

For a moment, it feels like a prank. What is he doing asking me out? I glance around to see if there's anyone waiting in the wings to laugh with him about this, but no one seems to pay that much attention to us.

"Sure." I'm surprised that this is happening, but willing to see where it goes.

"Cool, do you need to grab anything from your locker, or are you good to go?"

I throw my tote over my shoulder and shut my locker door. "I'm good."

"Great."

We walk in silence down the hallway. Oh gosh, is this awkward? Maybe he already regrets asking me out to lunch. I should say something.

"So -"

"I was -"

We both pause after talking at the same time.

"Go ahead." I say after a moment.

"I was just going to say that I was wondering what you're here for."

"Well, that's a philosophical question." He laughs.

"I meant, what's your specialty at school?"

I join him in laughing. "Ah, that makes more sense. I'm here for the IB program, but I got in for visual art as well. I like to design clothes. You?"

"I'm here for visual art as well, but photography. I love capturing a moment in time, freezing it almost, for posterity. It gives me such a high."

"I like that. It's cool to hear the perspective of the person behind the camera. Normally, I'm in front of it." I wince. Shoot, I hadn't meant for that to slip out. I probably sound conceited.

"In front of it?"

I sigh. "I model part-time. I've been doing so since I was in late elementary school."

"I can see why. From a photographer's point of view, you're perfect."

Wow, I'm so glad that he can't see the blush warming my cheeks.

"Oh wait, I just said that out loud, didn't I?" He looks chagrined.

"Yes, you did." I confirm, holding back a laugh. "I feel flattered by that comment, though. Unless you want to take it back? That might hurt my feelings a little, but

I'm a big girl. I'll survive."

He laughs, albeit nervously. "I don't want to take it back. I'm just not used to this."

"This?"

"Being so nervous around a girl that I say everything that pops into my head." Then he shakes his head. "And I just did it again."

"I make you nervous?"

"Very."

"How so?"

"I don't know. Maybe it's how beautiful you are. Or that you're so quiet that it gives off an air of mystery and that's a bit intimidating."

Beautiful? Mystery? Intimidating?

"I promise that I'm not as interesting as you probably think I am."

"Or, you're more interesting than you think you are," He counters.

"For real, ask me anything and I'll answer it. Then you'll see that I'm not that mysterious."

"So, like Truth or Dare, but without the dare?"

I laugh at his description. "Yes, just Truth I guess."

"Oh boy. You're going to regret giving me so much power." He teases and I laugh.

"We'll see."

"Okay, what's your ethnic background?"

Well, that's a simple question. "I'm Haitian."

"Oh wow! So am I; half-Haitian and half-Jamaican." I try to put on my best surprised face, as if I don't already know this about him. "It's rare to find us in the GTA. Most of my Haitian side of the family is in Quebec."

"That's where I'm from. I only just moved here at

the beginning of the school year."

"That's a bit of a change, eh?"

"Yeah, it is." I can't hide the sadness in my voice.

"It sounds like coming here has been hard for you. Is that accurate?" I nod my head. "Would you like to talk about it more?" I shake my head. "Okay, then we'll change the topic. Tell me about your family."

"Well, it's just me, my manman and my stepdad, Don."

"No siblings?"

"Nopers, just me and the parents."

"I can't even imagine that. I have four siblings. Your house must be so quiet."

I laugh at how awestruck he sounds. "Well, you can come over sometime and see, I guess." The words are out of my mouth before I have a chance to think about it. Once it hits me what I said, I am mortified. Did I just invite him over? That's way too forward of me.

"Let me take you to lunch first and then see if you still want to give that invitation."

At the mention of lunch, I glance around, surprised to realize that we're already at the mall. "Speaking of lunch, where are we going? The food court is that way." I gesture to the left.

"Yeah, I'm trying to impress you, Gaelle. That means bringing you to an actual restaurant."

I smile at his teasing tone and his words. "Do we have time for that, though?"

"We might need to speed walk back, worst-case scenario. Is that alright with you?"

"I can live with that. I can also live with being a few minutes late."

"That's the Haitian in you coming out in full force." I can't help but laugh at those words. Such a stereotype, but also so true for me and my family, at least. "You good with Pickle Barrel?"

"Yep, works for me. I've never been."

"Losing your PB virginity is such a momentous occasion. I'm glad that I'm here for it." He winks, and a giggle erupts from me. Him mentioning my virginity, even of the restaurant kind, has me feeling tingly all over.

"You're hilarious."

"I'm glad that you think so."

"I do."

"Well, I didn't expect to hear those words from you so soon. We are underage, after all." It takes a moment for me to understand what he's said and then comes another giggle. "What? I'm serious! I could do far worse." He hams it up, and I shake my head, still giggling.

"That's what every girl longs to hear, Josué."

"Are you saying that was a bad proposal? Let me try again." He falls down on one knee and reaches for my hand.

"Will you, Gaelle last-name," I snort at this, and he gives me a satisfied grin, a devilish glint in his eyes, "make me the happiest guy alive and -"

"Were you guys hoping for a table?" We both turn towards the direction of the impatient sounding voice and see a hostess with an unamused look on her face.

Josué stands up and gives her a warm smile. "Yes, please."

"Right this way." She turns around, and we follow her to a booth.

"Your waiter will be with you soon."

We both nod and smile at her and then exchange an amused glance with each other.

"Why do you think she was so upset?" I ask him.

"Maybe she has a boyfriend that she's waiting to propose and seeing me doing that for you triggered her."

I nod my head. That would make sense. "That's pretty insightful, Josué."

"I love the way you say my full name. Your French accent is sexy."

Oh boy, here comes the blushing again. Time for a subject change. "Hey, remember we were playing Truth? Have you learned everything you want to know about me?"

He looks at me, aghast. "Are you kidding? We've barely scratched the surface. I want to know everything about you."

"Everything?"

"Everything." His voice is firm.

"That would take longer than this lunch break allows."

"You're adorable. As if I'm not hoping to have more time with you than this."

My cheeks are warming again. I'm so glad that he can't see how much he makes me blush. "How much more time?"

"The rest of our lives, if that's what it takes."

"You're putting on your A-game, eh?" I sidestep the seriousness of his words with some teasing.

"I'm just choosing to embrace the lack of filter that I seem to have with you. Life's too short to not go for it."

Underneath his confidence, I detect something sad. "It feels like you've had to come to terms with the shortness of life in a hard way."

For the first time in our time together, he looks away. When he meets my eyes again, his are teary.

"Oh Josué, what happened?"

"My dad died last year of a heart attack. The paramedics weren't able to get there in time." I reach across the table and hold out one of my hands. He takes it immediately.

"I'm so, so, so sorry. Did you guys have a good relationship when he passed?"

"We did. He was my hero. He was a teacher back in Haiti but came here and worked a blue-collar factory job to provide for us. He was funny and kind. Of course, sometimes we butted heads, but mostly, we were a vibe. I miss him every day."

"He sounds like an amazing man."

"He was." I don't know what else to say, so I opt for silence and move my thumbs softly over his knuckles. "I did not intend to cry on this date." He says after a moment.

"Tears are always okay." This makes him smile for the first time since his dad was brought up.

"Thanks. Tell me about your dad."

"Oh, well. I haven't seen him in nine years. My mom and I caught him cheating on her, and I haven't seen him since that day. I believe my mom got full custody of me in the divorce, and that's that." I try to say it all casually, but there's still hurt in my voice.

"That sucks. I hate what happened to your family. You deserved better." The adamance in his voice feels like it's giving my heart a hug.

"Thank you. I would say cheers to our moms for persevering through trials, but we don't have any drinks yet."

He laughs at this. "We are going to be so late for class, aren't we?" I join him in his laughter. "Well, I would say this time with you is more than worth it." He says and squeezes my hand gently. I glance down at our hands in surprise. I forgot they were still together. It just feels so natural now to be this connected to him.

"Agreed." My response earns me a full smile from him.

We sit in companionable silence for a moment, our thumbs doing a waltz together.

"Oh man, how are we going to eat with only one hand each?"

The dismay on his face makes me laugh. "Here's an idea: we could, you know, just stop holding each other's hands when the food comes. Whenever our mythical waiter shows up, that is."

He smiles at that, and then his face gets serious. "But I don't think I want to let go of you."

I'm touched by his words. "You'll get it back when our food is done. That's a promise."

And when we leave the restaurant an hour later, I keep it, because here's a little secret: I didn't want to let go of him either.

Chapter 3

That night, we spend hours talking on Instagram, sending videos back and forth. I can't remember the last time I laughed so much. Before saying goodnight, he invites me out to have lunch with him again and I, of course, say yes.

The next morning, I make up an hour earlier to get ready. It takes forever to find the clothes I used to wear and then figure out what to do with my hair. In some ways, it feels nice to put effort into my appearance again. In other ways, it feels a bit scary; like, since I'm not invisible anymore, people can reject me.

Then again, as long as Josué accepts me, no one else's rejection even matters.

When I walk into school, I am pleasantly surprised to see him waiting for me at my locker. He ogles me, making me feel good about the burgundy sweater dress that I decided upon.

"You look beautiful, Gae." His voice has a breathy tone, and that paired with a nickname warms my insides.

I smile at him. "Thank you. You look great, too." Well, he always did to me. Today, in a charcoal grey button down and black cardigan, is no exception.

"I'm not too proud to admit that I was dressing to impress you today." He responds with a wink.

Does he know how irresistible he looks when he does that? How it can unsettle its recipient? Before I can respond, the warning bell goes off. "Shoot." I mutter to myself as I grab what I need for the morning and then close my locker.

"May I walk you to your class?" Why do these words sound more meaningful than they should be? It feels like he's inviting me into something daring and intimate all at once. Overcome by emotions that I cannot explain, I nod my head.

Then he reaches for my hand. In my surprise, I nearly drop my books, which doesn't escape his notice. "Is this okay?"

"Mhmm." My heart feels like it's beating so loud that I'm surprised he can't hear it.

He gives my hand a gentle squeeze. "So, where are we headed?"

Oh, right! He doesn't know my schedule.

"Math with Ms. Kaminska."

"Gotcha. Let's go. I remember her being a stickler for punctuality."

As we walk together, my nerves dissipate at the comfort of just being close to him. Yes, I do not know what's happening between us or what he's thinking regarding me, but I still feel safe with him despite all that uncertainty. And holding his hand is like a tangible reminder of that safety.

When we arrive at my class, I push down the disappointment at being separated from him.

"I'll see you at lunchtime. Are you okay if I meet you at your locker again?"

I clear my throat, afraid that I might otherwise squeak. "That works for me."

"Cool. I've gotta run. See you later."

I do a little wave and then walk to my usual seat. Lunch can't come fast enough.

~

It's time to see Josué. It felt like the last few hours dragged by and like lunch would never come. Is this normal, this needing to be with the person you like all the time?

When I get to my locker, I make quick work of dumping my books. I don't want to lose any time with him. It was for naught though, since after a few minutes, he still wasn't here.

Was this all a prank and I'm now being stood up?

I force myself to breathe. There are so many reasons he'd be late. He could've needed to poop for all I know. I should give him the benefit of doubting my fears. Then I feel a gentle tap on my shoulder and turn around to see him grinning at me wearing a large backpack. My fears disappear. He showed up. He still wants to spend time with me.

"Ready to go?" He asks me.

"Yes."

He takes my hand once more and we walk down the hall together and out of the school. It is gorgeous outside, the sky a beautiful blue and the sun out in all its glory. It's nearing the end of November, and I haven't needed my winter jacket yet. That's crazy.

I walk on the path to the mall, but Josué stops me. "I have another place where we can have lunch." he has a mischievous glint in his eye. I could fall in love with that glint.

"Lead the way."

I follow him down another path I've never taken before, and it leads to this bridge over a little stream of clear water surrounded by trees. It is, like, 5 minutes away from our school and I've never heard of it before.

I take in the sight before me and breathe deeply. It's such a peaceful place. I turn to tell Josué how beautiful this place is and see him laying a blanket out on the grass and then placing croissants, chocolate chip cookies, ginger ale, a few slices of pizza and some chicken wings on the blanket. He even takes out plates and cups and napkins.

"Josué?" He glances up at me and flashes me a big smile.

"I thought we could have a picnic today."

I am touched. This is so thoughtful. I sit down on the blanket beside him.

"Well, let's dig in."

I don't need to be told twice. I fill my plate with a slice of pizza and 3 chicken wings while he pours our ginger ale into cups.

"So, how did you even get this food?" I ask.

"I ordered it from the Caf. They made the cookies and croissants fresh this morning and the pizza and chicken wings just about 20 minutes ago. That's why I was a bit late at your locker. I was picking up the food."

My heart melts. The cafeteria is crazy expensive. Him spending so much money on this date is flattering but also appalling. My face must betray my feelings.

"You're worth what this cost."

This is too perfect. Good things like this didn't happen to me.

"But why? Why have you suddenly taken an

interest in me? Why are you acting like you like me?" I am frustrated and waiting for the other shoe to drop. There has to be a catch here.

He glances at me to check if I am as serious as my tone indicates. And then he just says nothing. My heart thumps wildly, the beat ringing through my ears. And my thoughts follow its tempo. Beat. He doesn't like me. Beat. He was playing with me. Beat. I've made a terrible fool of myself.

"Since you won't answer my question, I think that I'll go. You can screw with someone else's life. I'm not interested." I stand and walk away.

"No! Wait!" So those vocal cords are working?

He comes to me and holds my hands in his, making direct eye contact with me. My breath catches at all the feelings I see in them.

"The reason I didn't answer your question was because it would be embarrassing. It wasn't because you don't matter to me, or that I'm playing with you. Back in September, I was interested in you. That day when you looked a little lost, and I gave you directions where to go?" He pauses, and I nod to show that I remember that day.

"When I saw you, you were just perfect. Your sweatpants and disdain for being here weren't enough to hide how beautiful you are. But I was a coward. I told my friends that I was thinking of asking you out, and they talked me out of it, not seeing what I saw; what I see. So, I didn't act on my crush. When I saw you yesterday, it was like you had stopped hiding, and I knew other guys would be quick to ask you out, so I took the chance and invited you to lunch. And I had even more fun with you than I thought I would."

My heart flutters at his words, but my mind is skeptical. Is this true? Did he find me beautiful before yesterday? Is he interested in me?

Suddenly, a breeze goes by and blows a couple of my faux locs into my face. He pushes them behind my ear, his touch tender. Instinctively, I lean into his touch. My mind may be in one place, but my body is in another. It trusts him.

Suddenly, his face is only a few centimetres away and then his lips gently press against mine.

Time stops.

My body somehow feels more alive now than it ever has felt, almost like I've only been existing and now I'm living. When he pulls away from me, I know that something incredible has just happened. Something that I'm not sure I'm able to explain. Something good. Something real. I no longer doubt his feelings are true.

"That was another chance I took. Did I blow it?" His voice is nervous.

"Just the exact opposite." I lean forward to kiss him in return.

By the time lunch is over, our food has barely been touched.

Chapter 4

"Elle!"

"Thia!"

My best friend and I greet each other enthusiastically, as if it's been longer than a week since we've had our Skype catch up time. Even though I live much closer to her than before we moved, it's still a couple hours on transit for either of us to get to the other, so we resort to Skype.

"Ma soeur, comment ça va?"

I smile at her attempt at incorporating French for my sake. "Truthfully, it's been a crazy week."

Her eyebrows raise in surprise at my response. "Don't leave your girl in suspense! What happened?"

"I may have gone on a couple dates and made out with the most popular guy in the 12th grade?" It comes out like a question, partly because it still feels crazy that all of this happened.

Her mouth falls open.

"Rewind. Who is he? What dates? Was this your first kiss? Why am I just now hearing of this?"

"I wanted to see you react."

She snorts at this explanation. "Oh, I'm reacting all right."

"His name is Josué."

"French?"

"Half-Haitian."

"What's his last name?"

"You want to creep him, eh?"

"Of course."

I laugh at this. "Désulmé. He's a year older than us and a photographer."

"I'm on his profile now." I can see her on her phone. "Okay, he's fine! You better get that, soeur!

"You are too much, Thia!"

"You're welcome. Now, what were the dates?"

"We've gotten lunch together just about every day this past week. First, at a restaurant. The second was a picnic. The other two times were chill, just Burger King and McDonald's."

She nods in approval. "I can respect that. He has to be wise with his funds. Assuming that he's been paying for things?"

"He has. I want to tell him he doesn't have to do that, but I don't know how."

"It will come up at the right time. For now, just roll with it."

I nod at the wisdom. "Thanks. And yes, it was my first kiss - but I've lost count how many there's been with him since." I duck my head in embarrassment as Ruthia laughs.

"Oh my gosh, I am so living vicariously through you right now. Lord knows, nothing is happening in my life in this department."

"You like a guy at your church, right? Shawn is the name coming to mind, but I know that's not right."

"You're close, it's Shane." She sighs. "It's

becoming clear to me, though, that he won't see me as anything but as a sister. I'm not model beautiful like you, Gaelle. No guy ever thinks of me that way."

My heart pangs. I hate the way my best friend talks about herself sometimes. Like, she is beautiful. Even with the braces and glasses. But she doesn't believe me when I tell her so.

"Anyway, you like him?"

"I do. He's funny and smart and makes me feel seen and safe." It's not until the words leave my mouth that I realize how true they are.

"You're falling in love with him!"

"We've only spent time together four times. It's way too early for the L word."

"Fair enough. But you really like him, eh?"

"Yeah, I really do."

She squeals at my response. "I'm going to bring up this conversation at your wedding."

I shake my head at her antics but can't help but hope that she's right, that this is my fairytale unfolding. "So, tell me about your week, Thia? I don't want to hog the whole time."

She sobers up. "Well, last night at Youth group got a little intense."

My curiosity is piqued. My mom and Don have never been religious. I only went to church with my granmè back in Montreal, but I've never been to a youth group before. Whenever Ruthia tells me stories about it, I'm always interested. "How so?"

"Well, he preached a message on Genesis 3. You know, after Adam and Eve sin, then hide from God?"

I nod, familiar with what she's sharing.

"Well, God asks them where they are. Our youth

pastor leaned into that. He said that God knew where they were, but he asked them that question for them to realize where they were at spiritually."

"That's deep."

"Right? And then he asked us the same question: where are we in our relationships with God? It got me thinking. How are God and I? Am I okay with it? Does our relationship need to change?"

"Those are legit questions, Thia. You've got me thinking too." I pause for a moment. "Where do you think you're at in your beliefs?"

"Well, I believe in God. And, I believe that if I live a good life and do the right things, then God will be happy with me and I'll be okay."

"That sounds reasonable to me. That's what religion is for, right? Being a good person."

"What about you, Elle?" She asks.

"I definitely think that there's, like, a spiritual … dimension to life. And if we want to call that 'God', I'm good with that. I just don't see why it's such a big deal, though. Like, why would my granmè dedicate so much time, energy and money to this?" I shrug.

"Hmm. I think I can understand where you're coming from. Maybe it's something that we'll understand when we're older. Why God is such a big deal to people, I mean."

"You might be right, Thia. In the meantime, I think I'm good at where I am. You?"

She sighs. "I'm still figuring things out, Elle. But when I'm good, you'll be the first to know." She smiles at me, and I smile back. I'm so thankful to God - or whoever - for Ruthia.

Chapter 5

"I'm so glad that you've come out of your shell, Gaelle." Manman says to me as she passes me the container of Riz collé ak pois [rice and red beans].

It shouldn't surprise me that she's noticed my changes. In the last week, I have been dressing better and smiling more, but I guess I thought she was so wrapped up in Don and work that it would slip her regard.

"Mèsi [*thank you*] manman." Should I tell her about Josué? Before our move, it wouldn't have been a question, but things feel different between us now.

"What changed for you?"

Well, I have to tell her now or lie. I take a deep breath. "Actually, there's a boy at school that …" oh shoot. Are we dating? We haven't really gone out on actual dates, only lunch ones. "I've been spending time with." I finally land on.

Manman and Don exchange a surprised look.

"Oh. Well, way to bury the lead there, Gaelle." Don jokes and I chuckle.

"Tell us about him." My manman says, her tone inviting.

"Well, he's half-Haitian and funny and a talented

photographer. We've been eating lunch together." And kissing, but they don't need to know that.

"Well, he sounds nice. I would like to meet him sometime." Manman says. She sounds curious, not judgy in any way.

"Okay. We'll set something up. I think you'll like him a lot." I mean my words, but a bit of worry comes over me. Meeting the parents is a big deal, right? Maybe we're not there yet. We haven't even hung out outside of school!

Once dinner is done and the table is cleared, I head upstairs to my room and go on my phone. I laugh at the funny video that Josué sent me and respond with a few emojis.

I almost drop my phone when I see a call coming from him. He's never called me before. What does this mean? I answer the call, and my nerves disappear once I see his smiling face.

"Hey Gae." His voice is so warm.

"Hey Josué. You called?" I mentally face palm myself. Way to state the obvious, Gaelle.

"Yeah, I just realized that I'd rather see your face and hear your voice live rather than over text."

His words only make me relax more, and I settle into my bed. "Is this your way of saying that you missed me?" My voice is a mix of teasing and flirty, and it earns me a laugh from him.

"That's it. I've loved our lunch dates, but that's just not enough time with you for me. Does that make me sound clingy?"

"Not at all. I've been feeling the same way. What do you have in mind?"

His smile stretches across my screen, and I feel a

bit of awe that I'm the one who made him that happy. "Well, do you like to bowl?"

"I haven't done it in ages. But I'm game."

"How does Saturday afternoon sound to you?"

Like two days too far away.

"I need to check with my manman, but it should be fine." That reminds me of dinner. "Oh! She wants to meet you." At this, his eyebrows raise, and I rush to explain. "I sorta mentioned you at dinner tonight." Oh Gawd. This is embarrassing. What if he thinks I'm into this, like more than he is? "I didn't say you were my boyfriend, though." Maybe that will smooth it over.

Now, though, he looks upset. Crap. I went about this all wrong.

"Gaelle, if you don't want me to be your boyfriend, then please let me know. I thought with all the time we've been spending together, we were together. But I guess not."

I'm utterly taken aback by the agony in his tone. "We just never talked about it, so I didn't want to assume. Of course, I want to be your girlfriend."

His eyes brighten, but his facial expression is still skeptical. "You're sure?"

"One thousand percent sure."

"Great. Well, girlfriend, I would be happy to meet your mom and stepdad. I want to see who's made you to be as great as you are."

I smile at this, but nerves still tug at me. "You're sure you don't feel like it's too soon?"

"Positive. How about I come over a bit earlier than when we have to leave? Then there's time for your mom to interrogate me." His joking tone relaxes me a tad bit.

"Okay, boyfriend. That sounds like a plan to me."

He gives me a big grin. "I don't think I'll ever tire of you calling me that."

"Good, because I plan to say it to you often."

"No complaints here. But, umm, maybe we should talk about our expectations for this relationship? Now that we're official?" He sounds nervous, so I give him an encouraging smile.

"That sounds really wise. It must be that extra year that you have on me." I tease, and he laughs.

"It's just that I've had girlfriends before, and they've been upset that I didn't do certain things for them or with them, and I don't want that to happen with you."

"Oh." He's the first boyfriend that I've had. I have nothing to compare him to, but he has these other girls to compare me to. That realization is like someone has dumped cold water onto my head.

"Yeah, so what would make you feel cared for by me?"

I take a moment to think about it. "Honestly, just spending more time together. Maybe you introducing me to your friends?"

"Those sound doable to me. I like our lunch dates, but I go to the library after school to work with a few friends. You could join me one day next week and see if it's something that you'd be into."

"That is a great idea. I'll join you Monday then."

"Great. But is there anything else? Do you want flowers and chocolates or brief notes in your locker?"

"Those all sound nice in theory, but I'm just content to have time together. Maybe we could agree that we'll see each other in person at least once on a weekend?"

"Are you sure that's all you want?"

"Yep, for now, at least. I'll keep you posted. Is there anything that I can do for you?"

He looks taken aback by the question. "Nothing that you're not already doing."

"Well, that's good to hear!"

"Umm, what about physically?"

"Physically?" I'm confused.

"Like, are you comfortable doing more than kissing one day, or do you just want things to remain as they are?"

Oh. I have to think about that. It's not like I'm saving myself for marriage or anything, but I want to have sex with a guy that I feel loves me.

"I'm open to more as our relationship progresses? I know that's a vague answer but -"

"- that's a great answer." He assures me. "Well, like, not a great answer in that if you said something else, it would be a bad answer, just that I'm glad that you're willing to share where you're at with me. Kay, I'm going to stop. I'm babbling."

I can't help but laugh at his word vomit. "It's okay. You're cute when you babble. It shows me you're not just this super suave guy. You being unfiltered around me, even to your detriment, has been endearing from day one."

"I swear, you're the only girl I've met to bring that out of me."

"I must be special or something."

His face takes on a more serious look. "You are, Gaelle. You really are."

Oh boy, when he looks at me like that. It's like I

can't even think. It just makes me want to be near him. Him being on a screen makes him seem way too far away.

Chapter 6

I wipe my sweaty palms on my jeans as I wait for Josué to arrive. I'm not even nervous about our date. I'm nervous about him meeting my mom. She seems way too chill reading a book in the armchair. What does she have planned to ask him?

When the doorbell rings, I startle and then jump up. "I'll get it, manman."

She gives me a bemused look as she puts her book down. "Okay, Gaelle."

I walk over to the front door and open it to see a beautiful Black woman on the other side. I'm confused for a moment until I see Josué's eyes in her face. This must be his mom.

"Good afternoon Mme Désulmé. My name is Gaelle. Please, come in." I use my most polite tone and give her what I hope is a confident smile and move out of the way. Behind her is Josué, looking very apologetic.

He leans closer to me and whispers. "I'm so sorry. I meant to take a taxi here, but she insisted on coming because she wanted to meet you and your mom."

"That's okay. It's great to see you, regardless." I whisper back, itching to give him a kiss on the cheek but thinking better of it when I consider our moms are present. When their shoes are off, I direct them to follow me into the living room.

"Manman, this is Mme Désulmé and Josué." My mom rises from her seat to shake their hands.

"You may call me Lorraine," Mme Désulmé says to manman.

"And I'm Béatrice. It's a pleasure to meet you, under surreal circumstances. Please sit." My manman gestures to the couches in the room.

I move to sit on the loveseat, assuming that Josué and his mom will sit on the three-seater, but he sits beside me instead. I gawk at him in surprise.

"Surreal indeed. I just can't believe my baby boy is dating someone."

"Right? It feels like just yesterday I was teaching her how to walk."

"Or getting him to breastfeed! He had a tongue tie, you know, so it was difficult."

"Gaelle had the same issue! I remember how frustrating it was, first birth and then not even this could go well." My manman commiserates.

"You had a crappy birth experience, too?"

"Oh yeah, after 20 hours of labour and Gaelle's heartbeat dropping, we had to have an emergency C-section. And it took three times for them to get the epidural in correctly."

His mom gasps. "No!"

"Yes! I was terrified! I'm just glad that she got here safely in the end."

"Amen to that! With Jo-jo, I had decided that I wanted to do it at home with midwives."

"You didn't?"

"Oh, I did. Yeah, not the best decision for me. It took 36 hours of labour for him to come." Mme Désulmé shakes her head. "Oh, how I wished for an epidural! That pain was the worst I've ever felt. I've never forgotten it."

My mom laughs. "I know that's right."

Is this really happening? Are they just trading birth stories and talking about us like we're not even here? I don't know whether to be happy that they're getting along and the focus is off us or if all that's being shared should embarrass me.

"So, I must ask. Where did you get your hair done? Those twists are everything!" Mme Désulmé says to my manman.

"Oh, I do them myself. Mine and Gaelle's. We just crochet it in."

"How much do you charge? I would love to try that style myself."

"Oh, no charge at all! It doesn't take very long, especially if we put on a good movie."

"I'll hold you to that," Mme Désulmé teases and the two laugh together.

"I guess we should discuss our kids dating, eh?" my manman says when their laughter dies down.

"If we must." They turn their attention to us.

"Josué, I would love to know your goals for your future." My manman starts.

"I would love to know the same about Gaelle." Mme Désulmé adds.

Josué clears his throat. "Well, I hope to grow in my skills as a photographer and do that professionally. I'm not yet sure whether that will be in advertising or weddings or some other field, but that's what I want to do. I also have an aptitude for engineering that I'm going to pursue as well."

I search my manman's face for how she feels about his answer, but she gives nothing away.

"And you, Gaelle?"

"Oh, right! I want to be a doctor. I love kids, so a pediatrician or family doctor is most likely what I want to do."

"Oh, that's wonderful to hear!" she exclaims, and I relax.

I glance at my manman again and see that she's wearing a big smile on her face. I nailed it.

"And what are your intentions with dating my daughter, Josué?"

I nearly cover my face in embarrassment. Did she really just ask him that? I glance at him to see how he feels about the question, and he catches my gaze. He smiles at me and takes one of my hands in his and gives it a light squeeze. Then, he turns his attention to my manman.

"I think your daughter is wonderful. I want to keep getting to know her better and I hope that I'll have the privilege of doing that for a long, long time."

I can't stop the smile that his words cause. My manman smiles too. "Well, that's definitely an acceptable answer. Don't you think so, Lorraine?"

"I do, Béatrice. We should let these kids get to their date."

I breathe a sigh of relief. It's over and everything went okay.

"Do you guys need a ride?" My manman asks.

"No, Mrs. Louissaint, I'm planning to order an Uber to take us there and back - if that's okay."

"That's fine with me. Lorraine, do you have plans today?" And with that, it's like we're not even in the room anymore as our moms decide to spend the afternoon together.

Chapter 7

"Should I be worried that our moms just get along so well?" I say jokingly to Josué as we enter the Uber, making him laugh.

"Honestly, I'm about it. I think that went well, and it's good for them to be friends. One day, they may even become family." He winks.

I feel my face warm. "Are you implying marriage right now?"

"Didn't I already propose to you on our first date?" He volleys back and I laugh.

"Oh my gosh, that feels like ages ago. And it's only been a couple of weeks."

"I know what you mean. It's hard to remember what life was like before us." I smile at his words, glad that I'm not the only one feeling this way. He reaches for my hand and squeezes it, sending tingles up my arm.

I squeeze back and lean my head against his shoulder. "I really like you, Josué Désulmé."

I can feel him relax even more at my words. "Same here, Gaelle. Same here."

We sit like that in a comfortable silence for the rest

of the ride to the bowling alley. When we arrive, we thank our driver and then head inside. The lighting is low, and it takes a moment for me to adjust. On the right is an arcade, on the left is an area to order food and in front of us, wall to wall, are different lanes for bowling. Music is blasting from the speakers, and excited voices permeate the space.

"This is so cool!"

Josué smiles at my enthusiasm. "Right? We're headed this way." He points to a desk by the entrance of the arcade and I nod.

We're lucky that there isn't a line at the desk. "Hi, I reserved a lane for two under Joe." His voice is polite to the woman behind the desk.

"Just give me a sec." She scans the monitor screen in front of her. "Yep, I see it. And you already paid online, so I just need your shoe sizes and then you'll be good to go in lane 19."

"I'm a size 9." I tell her.

"I'm a size 11 and a half."

I look up at him in shock. "Your feet are enormous!"

He just laughs. "You know what they say about men with big feet."

"Okay there, Big Foot, don't gas yourself up."

"Wow." He draws out the word, making me giggle. "That's how it is? Okay, okay."

"I'm going to call you BF from now on."

"For Big Foot, I'm presuming?"

"Yes. And for boyfriend." I give him a quick kiss on the cheek to soften the blow of all my teasing.

"Okay, nickname accepted. Let's go to our lane."

"Aye aye, BF." I mock salute, and he laughs again.

We walk over to lane 19 and it's a relief that we don't have anyone beside us on either side. It affords us a bit more privacy in such a loud and crowded space.

"When's the last time you went bowling again?" He asks me.

"Umm. Early elementary school, like grade two maybe? I barely remember it."

"Okay, well, first we have to choose our names for our turns. It doesn't have to be our actual names. It can be anything."

"Well, yours should be BF."

He laughs. "Okay, but that means that I get to choose yours."

"Go for it. I'm curious to see what you'll come up with."

He pauses for a moment, looking deep in thought and then types in: 'Hottie'. I burst out laughing.

"Really, BF?"

He shrugs. "All I could think about was how beautiful you are, but beautiful is too long a word."

What am I supposed to say to that? "That's sweet, Josué."

"I have my moments. Now let's bowl!" His childlikeness makes me smile.

He tests out a few balls, walks up to the lane, and bowls a strike.

"I didn't realize that I was in the presence of greatness!"

"It was a lucky bowl." He sounds embarrassed.

"I doubt that." I mimic what he did with trying different balls, but they all feel too heavy for me.

"Need a lighter ball?" He asks. I nod, and he's off to another lane to grab me a few more to try.

The 7lb one that he brings over is perfect for me.

"Now, how do I do this? The last time I bowled, I'm pretty sure that I just put it between my legs and released it with both hands. I also had a barrier up so that it wouldn't go into the gutter."

"Yeah, that won't do. I gotchu, babe." Something in me flutters at the term of endearment. "First, let's make sure that you're holding the ball correctly. Place your thumb in this hole and your middle finger and ring finger in these holes." I follow his directions. "Great, now let's walk up to the foul line. This is the line that you don't want to cross." We walk to the line together. "You're going to want your left foot to be ahead of your right foot." He drops and adjusts my feet. "And then you swing your arm to throw the ball." I look at him dubiously, and he chuckles. "Okay, I'll help you with the swing."

He stands behind me, my back against his chest and his head just above my right shoulder. He puts his hand near mine and guides my hand backwards and then forwards. "Now, release." He whispers and I let go, closing my eyes at the intimacy of the moment. I'm so consumed by his nearness that I don't even realize that all the pins were knocked down until he roars. "You did it!"

I open my eyes to see that I've also gotten a strike. "I've decided that I want you to help me with each round, just like this."

"Nah, that was way too hot for me to do that multiple times. I've gotta keep it PG, hottie. There are kids around." This makes me laugh. I'm glad that I'm not the only one who was affected by that moment. "Plus, I need my hands for documentation." I raise my eyebrows at this and understanding dawns as he takes a camera outside of his satchel.

"You want to take pictures of us bowling?"

"Yeah, I wish I had remembered it on our first two lunch dates, but that's fine. We can make up for it. Are you okay with your picture being taken? I assumed yes because of your part-time job, but it just hit me. I shouldn't have assumed." He sounds nervous, so unlike his self-assured self.

"Chill Josué, I'm good with it." I assure him, and he relaxes.

"Cool, well, let's get bowling!"

And with that, we're off. I actually knock some pins down with his pointers, and he encourages me all the way, snapping pictures here and there. We finish one game pretty fast and then decide to get something to eat. Once we return to our lane with pizza and drinks, we tuck into our food.

"So, I had an idea, but I'm okay if you don't want to do it."

"Enough with the suspense, BF. Lay it on me." I wince at my words as soon as they're out of my mouth, not intending them to be so laced with sexual innuendo.

"I read this article on the New York Times website about these questions that lead to people falling in love. Are you down to answer them with me? Kind of like extending our game of Truth?"

"Are you asking me to fall in love with you?" I respond in a teasing voice, and he laughs.

"Like you're not already on your way there, hottie." He teases back and now it's my turn to laugh.

"Okay, how many are there?"

"Let me check." He takes out his phone and swipes

a few times. "Thirty-six."

I'm surprised at the number. "That's a good amount of questions but doesn't seem enough for something as big as love."

"I know right! That's why I'm curious to try them and see if it works."

His enthusiasm is adorable and contagious. "Well, I'm game. What's the first question?" I ask him.

"Given the choice of anyone in the world, whom would you want as a dinner guest?" He reads off his phone.

My answer is immediate. "Michelle Obama. She's just the epitome of an excellent Black woman. Beautiful, intelligent, classy, ambitious. I just love her."

"Trust me, you're already on your way to being like her."

His words bring a shy smile to my face. "Thank you. How about you?"

"Andre Wagner. He's a Black photographer and is so talented. I would just love to learn about the craft from him."

I make a mental note to check out some of this guy's work, since he means so much to him.

"Next question, would you like to be famous? In what way? My answer to this is yes. I'd love to be famous for photography."

"That makes sense for you to say. I would say no, I'm okay with being unknown."

"You're not trying to be the next Tyra Banks?" He teases, and I roll my eyes.

"Nah, modelling is not that serious to me. What's the next question?"

"Before making a telephone call, do you ever

rehearse what you are going to say? Why?"

He takes a bite of his pizza while I respond. "Yes! I hate phone calls and often feel like I need to be prepared ahead of time. Oh gosh, I feel so seen right now by that question."

"I don't call people, so this question feels irrelevant."

"What about when you call me?"

"Oh, well, you're not people. You're different." I feel my face warm at his response.

"Alright, what would constitute a "perfect" day for you? I would go to one of the seven wonders and take photos there, try new foods, and go on an adventure in that place."

"I didn't know that you were so adventurous. I feel like my answer is the opposite. I would be back in Montreal. I'd go to my favourite bagel place, then spend the morning reading at Chapters, then get lunch at my favourite poutine spot, then hike Mt. Royal with some friends, and finish the day by having dinner alone with my mom."

"Your day has a good mix of time with people and alone time. I think it's solid."

"Thanks for not thinking that it's boring or basic."

"No problem. Alright, when did you last sing to yourself? Or, to someone else?" He asks.

"Oh, that's easy. This morning. I sing in the shower every day. It's part of my routine." I finish off my first pizza slice.

"I can't remember. I rarely sing because I do not have a pleasant voice."

"Why don't I believe you?" I can't imagine there being something that he isn't good at.

"Oh, I'll prove it to you. I'll sing the next song that plays through the speakers." He declares and I giggle.

"A serenade? Oh, my heart!"

"Just remember, you asked for it!"

We wait for the current song, Watch me Whip, to finish to see what he'll be singing. Just the Way You Are by Bruno Mars plays.

I notice he turns sombre for a moment and then seems to shake it off of himself. Before I know it, he's holding his phone like a microphone and belting out the lyrics, looking at me the whole time.

He really can't sing.

But his sincerity more than makes up for it.

I cheer him on as he sings and when the song ends, I'm not the only one that's clapping. A few people in neighbouring lanes applaud him, too. He does a playful bow in response, and it's like I can feel my heart expand with care for him. Unsure of what to do with the feelings welling up inside of me, I lean forward across the table and kiss him as soon as he sits down.

"Well, I might have to serenade you more often if that's the response I'm going to get."

I shove him playfully. "Oh, shut up. What's the next question?"

"If you could live to the age of 90 and keep either the mind or body of a 30-year-old for the last 60 years of your life, which would you want?"

"Oh, my mind." My answer is automatic.

"Same. My grandma has Alzheimer's, and it's been horrible seeing her forget her family. I never want that to happen to me."

I feel a bit of my heart break at what he shared. "Oh, Josué. That's awful. I'm so sorry." I reach for his hand. He squeezes mine.

"Thanks. Let's move on?"

"Sure. Go for the next question. See if it'll lighten the mood."

"Do you have a secret hunch about how you will die?"

We both look at each other and start laughing. "Just the thing to ease up the vibe: death!" I say through giggles, and he snorts at that. "Well, no, I do not have a hunch, but I have a way that I don't want to die. I don't want to die for a stupid reason, like slipping and falling in the shower."

He snorts again at my answer, making me giggle. "Only you could make me laugh while talking about death, Gaelle."

"A little-known skill that I have. Maybe it has resume potential?" I joke and he laughs again. "What about you?"

"My answer is less funny. I also have a way I don't want to die, and the first thing that comes to mind is death at the hands of the police. I'm so aware as a Black male that looks older than I am of how dangerous the police can be. I don't want to die because I fit a description of someone who committed a crime or because my race and gender make me out to be a threat, you know?"

His voice is a cross between angry and sad. I see the heart of so many Black men in him. "Josué, I hear you. I hate that you've even had to think about that."

"I mean, what's the alternative? Trayvon was only a couple of years older than us. Hoodies look different to me now."

"Facts." Is all I can say.

"Sorry that I keep making everything so heavy." He apologizes, and I shake my head.

"Oh, no, you don't. Don't you dare apologize for being real with me. I would take all the authentic and heavy things than those that are lighter but fake. Am I clear?"

He looks at me with something akin to awe on his face. "Crystal, hottie."

I laugh at the use of the nickname and nudge one of his feet with one of mine under the table. "Okay, next question please."

"As you wish."

"Okay, Wesley." I tease, making him laugh.

"Alright, Princess. Name three things you and your partner appear to have in common. Hmm, we're both Black."

"Yep, we're both Gen Z." I add.

"And we both don't have our bio fathers in our lives, although for different reasons."

"Nice. How many more do we have left?" I ask him, getting up from the table to stretch.

"Four more in this set, but we can bowl again if you want."

I think about it for a moment and then shake my head. "Nah, let's finish."

"That's my girl." I can't help but smile at the possessive pronoun use. *His* girl. It's not very feminist of me, but I love it. "For what in your life do you feel most grateful?"

"That's easy, My mom. I wouldn't know what I'd do without her."

"Same." He answers. "Okay, if you could change anything about the way you were raised, what would it be? Hmm. I think corporal punishment. I know my parents loved me, but I hate that they physically hurt me when I misbehaved. It made me afraid of them. I don't know, I just don't think that's how a kid should feel towards their parents. There's a difference between respect and fear."

"Straight facts. My parents didn't hit me, but that's because I didn't let myself get caught doing anything wrong - not that I was rebellious at all, either. Still, it's messed up that Black families tend towards that type of parenting. When I become a mom, I don't want to resort to that."

"Same. But, as a dad."

For a moment, my mind flies to us being parents together, and I have to give myself a mental shake. We are so far from that.

"For me, it would be my dad not having an affair. I feel like if that hadn't happened, my life would've turned out so much differently."

"That makes sense, Gaelle. Okay, the next one is a doozy, so I'm going to skip it for us to come back to after we finish our game. Is that alright with you?"

I smile at him checking in with me before deciding. "Sure, I trust you."

"Okay, then our last question before we get back to bowling is: If you could wake up tomorrow having gained any one quality or ability, what would it be?"

"Oooo. A superpower question? Teleportation. I would love to go anywhere, anytime, with minimal cost or energy."

"Sick. Mine would be telekinesis. Moving things with my mind sounds like a badman ting!"

"Oh my gosh. You had to go all Toronto mans just

now, didn't you?"

"Of course. Gotta represent. Brap! Brap! Brap." I dissolve into giggles at his gunshot sounds. They're so at odds with who he has shown himself to be that I just can't take it seriously.

"Wow." He draws out the word. "I see you mocking your mans." I can't help but keep giggling. He lifts his camera and snaps a few pictures of me losing it. "Cute." He says after a moment.

"Let's just get bowling." I say through my giggles, wiping tears away from my eyes.

"Sure thing, you're up first, hottie."

That nickname is growing on me.

Chapter 8

"**Oh my gosh**. I'm so excited." I say for the umpteenth time as we exit the Uber.

"I couldn't guess. Are you sure that you want to be here?" Josué deadpans as we walk past the Canada's Wonderland sign and I nudge him.

"It's just that I've been dying to come here. It was one of the few advantages to moving out here. But with not having friends here and Ruthia not being able to go, it just never panned out. But I love amusement parks. I'm a bit of an adrenaline junkie with roller coasters. Sorry, I've said this all before, haven't I?" I duck my head in embarrassment.

"You may have, but that's okay. I'm glad to be someone to give you an experience that you're guaranteed to enjoy. It's a win-win for me. I get to make my girlfriend happy and do something fun."

I smile at him, calling me his girlfriend. Will it ever become so familiar to me it ceases to influence my insides?

Surprisingly, it's not that busy and we're through the ticket counter and into the park. I mean, it is early December, so I would understand why there's not a ton of people here. But it's Winterfest! I thought that would draw people out. Well, their loss, my - I mean our - gain.

"Now, I did some research online on the rides with the highest thrill factor and made a list of the ones that I want to go on." I pull out my phone and show him my list.

He glances down at my phone and then smiles at me. "A woman on a mission. I love that. Okay, let me grab a map real quick, and then we can plot our way through."

We decide to start with the Behemoth and head in that direction. I'm so excited that I can barely feel the chill in the air. It doesn't hurt that Josué and I are holding hands. When we get to the ride, the wait time is about 25 minutes.

I groan in frustration.

"Hey, it's not that bad. In the summer, you can easily wait an hour to get on." Josué assures me.

I look at him. I'm sure my face is aghast. "That's crazy. It better be worth it."

"Oh, it is. And this gives us time to work through our list of questions."

"That's right! Let's see how many we can burn through while we're waiting."

"I'm loving the enthusiasm, Gae. Alright, last week we just about finished Set 1. Now, we're onto Set 2."

"Was bowling only a week ago?" I wonder aloud. Between hanging out with his friends after school, spending our lunches together, and talking to him before bed, it feels like we've lived so much life this past week.

"Yeah, it feels longer though, doesn't it?"

I nod. "Sorry for interrupting you. What's our first question from Set 2?"

"No problem. Okay, if a crystal ball could tell you the truth about yourself, your life, the future, or anything else, what would you want to know?"

"Hmm. I have to think about that for a moment. Myself, my life or my future…"

"I think myself. I would love to answer the question confidently: who am I? Right now, I don't think that I can."

"Okay, Désulmé with the depth! I see you, sir!" He laughs at my antics.

"I think for me, it would be my future. I don't need to know all the things that are going to happen to me, but I would love to know if I'm happy in the future."

He nods at me. "That's real talk. Alright, is there something that you've dreamed of doing for a long time? Why haven't you done it?"

"Oh! Travel to Haiti. I want to visit the homeland. The biggest reason I haven't done it is finances."

"Nice. I would love to do that too. Mine is skydiving. I'm not the legal age to do it yet."

At this moment, I feel such a kinship with him it's crazy. "I knew there was a reason that we were together. We're both adrenaline junkies. That's something on my bucket list!"

"Maybe we can do both things together someday."

I can only smile at the implication that we'll be together long enough for those things to happen.

"Next up, what is the greatest accomplishment of your life?"

"Maybe learning how to bowl?" We laugh together at that. "Honestly, I'm not sure yet if I have accomplished anything significant." I'm surprised that I feel comfortable enough to share that with him. "What about you?"

"For me, it would be surviving my dad's death." His voice cracks a bit, and he clears his throat. My heart swells in admiration for him.

"Oh Josué, that makes perfect sense. That is a tremendous accomplishment."

"Thanks, Gaelle. Alright, this may be our last one since we're close to the front now." Surprised, I look around to see that there's only a few people ahead of us. Time flies whenever I'm with this guy, I swear. "What do you value most in a friendship? I would say honesty. For me, lying is such a violation of trust. Like, it's hard to come back from that."

"You're right. On my end, it would be integrity; people being consistent between what they say and what they do. I can't take a hypocrite or someone talking out of both sides of their mouth. You know what I mean?"

"You don't like snakes."

I feel seen. "Facts." Is my only response and then we're off on the ride.

The next two rides there are no lines and we're the only ones on them. When we get to the Soaring Timbers ride, there are some people in front of us, and we have time for another couple of questions. I lean against him, and he wraps his arms around my middle.

I glance down at the phone in his hands and read off the next question. "What is your most treasured memory? Oh! Meeting Ruthia. I've told you about her. She's my best friend. We met at a Christian convention that my grandmother had dragged me to. I was in the kids' area and was content to be by myself and read my book. This was, like, in the first grade. Then Ruthia sat beside me and asked what I was reading. We bonded over our shared love of Junie B. Jones, and the rest was history. I can't imagine my life without her."

"I look forward to meeting her someday. I think she followed me on Instagram."

"Oh, she 100 percent did. She creeped you as soon as I told her about you." I say, laughing.

"That's the mark of a good friend right there."

"Right? Okay, for you. What's your most treasured memory, BF?" He chuckles at my use of his nickname.

"Honestly, just watching a movie with my parents when my dad was alive."

"Aww, that's sweet." I look down for the next question and wince. "Yikes, the next one is harder. What is your most terrible memory?"

"Definitely saying goodbye to my dad. He was lying on the living room floor, barely able to breathe. I can remember when he stopped breathing. It was awful." I can feel him shaking behind me and turn around to give him a big hug.

"Oh, Josué. I'm sorry."

He holds me tightly and I feel his head nod against mine. "Thanks. What about you?"

"For sure, discovering my dad's affair. I still get flashbacks sometimes of him in bed with that woman." I shudder, and Josué wraps an arm around me. I smile at him.

"Alright, you two can go in that section." The voice of the ride operator interrupts us, and we do as she says, sitting beside each other. As we're flipped upside down and moved back and forth, it feels like the awful memory is being flung off of me. When we disembark and I can get a good look at Josué, he looks more free as well.

"I needed that ride after that last question." I comment as we walk away.

"Same. Where to next?" He opens up the map, and I open my list.

"Ooh. Shockwave is on my list, and it's close to where we are." I say, gesturing to the map in his hands.

"Sounds good to me." He folds up the map and puts it back in his pocket, then reaches for my right hand. Even though gloves separate our hands, the intimacy still makes my heart flutter.

From Shockwave, to the Drop Tower, to the Leviathan, we scream and laugh and cling to each other and it's everything. Who knew that roller coasters were even more fun with a boyfriend?

When we get to Dragon Fyre, there's a bit of a line, so we pull out the questions again, wary this time though.

Josué breathes a relieved sigh. "The questions are a bit more chill. If you knew that in one year you would die, would you change anything about the way you are now living? Why?"

"Oh yes. I wouldn't want to be in school anymore. I would rather travel all over the world and experience different cultures." I answer easily.

"Same! Where do you want to visit?"

"Oh, hmm. France. I know they're the colonizers and all, but I still want to go there."

"That's fair, Gaelle. It's supposed to be beautiful." He squeezes my hand, and I smile at him. "I'm trying to reach Japan. I'm sort of into Anime and would love to visit its birthplace, you know?"

"That makes sense. The only Anime I can say that I was into as a kid would be Sailor Moon, basic but…" I shrug.

"Not basic at all. Tuxedo mask was goals." His enthusiasm makes me laugh.

"Mans was my first crush." We laugh together.

"I don't blame you. Okay, next question: What does friendship mean to you? For me, it's someone who knows you super well, like all your flaws and stuff, and still is in your life."

"That's beautifully put. I think for me it's when someone cares for you and wants good things for you. No petty jealousy or sabotage, you know what I mean?"

"Yep, that's real talk. Oh look, we're good to go on the ride. After this one, how would you feel about getting something to eat?"

Only now do I realize that I'm hungry. "That sounds good to me." I answer as we climb into the ride. It's not as intense as some others, but it's still a good time. We walk over to International Street, where there are different food stalls.

"What are you feeling for?" He asks me.

I spot a Beavertails stall and am drawn by the promise of a fried dough and cinnamon. "Ooh. Beavertails."

"Say less. We can grab something from there."

The line is pretty short and soon we're finding a place to sit, me with a classic cinnamon and him with a Hazel amour.

"I haven't had one of these in ages, it feels like." I say after my first big bite.

"I feel like we need more of these around. Like we

have so many Tim Hortons, and I don't mind that, but like, what if for every 4 Tim Hortons, we could have a Beavertails? That would be legit."

"I agree. Gosh, this is so good." I let out a moan as I take another bite and Josué's eyes seem to darken. Without warning, he leans forward and gives me a deep kiss. When we pull apart, I look up at him in surprise. "What was that for?"

"Maybe I wanted to have a taste of your Beavertail?"

I laugh at this. "You're hilarious, BF." I respond as I take another bite. "Hey, how many questions do we have left?"

"Ummm, let me check." He pulls out his phone and studies his screen. "Four. We've really gotten through these." I hear a hint of surprise in his voice.

"Let's go, team!" I say enthusiastically, and he laughs. "Let's try to finish them."

"Okay, first up: what roles do love and affection play in your life?"

"Well, my mom is very affectionate, always giving me hugs and kissing me on the face. I guess affection plays a comforting role in my life. You?"

"That's so interesting. I feel like we are not an affectionate family, but I've never doubted that I was loved."

"That's all that matters, as long as you know that you're cared for. What's the next question?"

"Alternate sharing something you consider a positive characteristic of your partner. Share 5 items. First off would be your smile. It's stunning."

I feel my face warm. "Thanks. For me, your height. It just makes me feel safe."

"Nice, the way you tease me. I love that you feel comfortable enough to do that."

"My second one is like yours. I appreciate your sense of humour. I laugh so much when we're together."

"Hmm. I think my third is your resilience. You've gone through so much with your dad and then moving far away from all that was comfortable to you. I just admire that you've emerged from those things still as great as you are."

Do not cry, Gaelle. I think to myself as his words wash over me. I've never thought of myself as resilient before. "I think your vulnerability is my third one. How you're so unfiltered with me and willing to share things relating to *your* dad and his passing means a lot to me."

"Don't go making me cry now, hottie." I can tell that he's trying to make his tone teasing, but I hear the hoarseness that my words have caused.

"You started it, BF, talking about resilience!" We laugh together.

"Alright, two more. I would say that I like the way you present yourself in how you dress. It's very classy. I will also say that you're a great listener. I appreciate that about you." His words touch me. It's nice that those things are noticed.

I think for a moment and then they come to me. "My last two for you would be that you're very polite, especially to people like waiters and stuff. And you're a very talented photographer."

"Thank you. Okay, how close is your family? Do you feel your childhood was happier than most other people's? Yeah, I had two parents who loved each other and loved me. It wasn't a perfect childhood, but it was a good one." It's like I can picture Josué with his siblings and parents having a fun and close childhood. For a moment, I feel a pang of envy. I wish I could've had that.

"With my dad's affair, I would say that kind of torpedoed my childhood, so no, it was not happier than most other people's. But I love the closeness I have, or at least had, with my mom."

"I'm curious about the verb tense change there, Gae. And it flows into the last question: how do you feel about your relationship with your mother?"

"These questions are just coming for me today! My gosh. Well, I guess I feel replaced in some ways by my stepdad. I think they're great together and I like him and all, but we don't have that same closeness anymore. Sometimes, I feel more tolerated than loved." I blink away a few tears that come as I verbalize something that I've only thought before.

Josué leans over the table and swipes away a tear that escaped. "I hate that you feel that way because you deserve to feel loved all the time. Your existence is a freaking gift to everyone who meets you, Gaelle. For real."

Where did this guy come from? How did he speak to my heart exactly what it needed to hear? Overcome by the feelings coming up in me, I can only nod to acknowledge what he said.

"For my relationship with my mom, it feels complicated. Like, I'm not just her son anymore. As the eldest boy, I've become the new man of the house. I hate having all this responsibility. Sometimes, I feel like I just need a break. Just time to be a teenage boy. I don't know. Am I even making sense?"

"You're making complete sense to me, Josué." He smiles his thanks.

We sit for a moment in silence, just staring at each other. I'm not sure how long we're like that until someone walks up to us and asks if we'll be done with our table soon.

"Sure, man. You can have it." Josué says good-naturedly, and we get up from our seats. He reaches for my hand, and I smile at our entwined fingers. These questions may be working, because I'm pretty sure I'm falling in love with him.

Chapter 9

My phone rings and I'm surprised to see that it's Josué. We just said goodbye to each other an hour ago.

Something must be up.

"Hey Josué, what's up?"

"I just caught Madeline smoking a cigarette."

His younger sister, who's only twelve? "What the heck? How?"

"She wasn't even being smart about it. She was smoking in her room, as if no one could smell it from the hallway."

I shake my head. "That's so bad for her. Smoking can lead to lung cancer!"

"I know! That's what I told her. It would be one thing if it were weed, but nicotine? Like, what in the world compelled her to think that was a good idea?"

"Facts. What was her response?"

"She said that I should stop trying to be dad." His voice goes from angry to hoarse.

"Oh Josué."

"Yeah, so then I left the house. I didn't want to say something that I would regret later. Can I come over?"

How level-headed of him. "Of course. I'll

reschedule with Ruthia."

"Nah, don't do that. I can just chill in the living room while you guys talk in your room."

"It's okay, I'll just see about chatting with her tomorrow. It sounds like you need me more right now."

"Thanks, Gaelle. I'll see you within the hour. I'm gonna bus."

"No worries. See you soon."

I shoot off a quick text to Ruthia that Josué is having an SOS moment and needs me, and she calls me right away.

"So, you love him!" Is how she starts the call.

I laugh. "What are you talking about?"

"You rain checking time with your best friend to care for him screams love to me."

"You're crazy. It's only been a few weeks that we've been together."

"Okay, then describe to me how you feel about him."

"Well, I … I.." every time I go to say the word 'like', it feels insufficient. Oh crap, maybe I love him.

"Told you." I can hear the self-satisfied smirk in her voice.

"It's just that he makes me feel seen and safe and adored. I laugh whenever we're together but also want to cry too. It doesn't matter what I'm doing. As long as I'm near him, I'm happy. Oh my gosh, is that love?"

"It very well sounds like it. I'm so happy for you, sis!"

"What if he doesn't love me back?"

"Well, you don't have to tell him soon. You can always wait for him to say it first."

"That's true." Relief washes over me. "Thank

you."

"You're welcome. Go, take care of your man! Let's talk Sunday afternoon?"

"Sounds like a plan. Bye Thia!"

"Bye!"

I hang up the call and stare at the phone in shock.

I'm in love with Josué.

Oh gosh, I want to tell him, but I don't want to risk him not feeling the same way yet. It's only been a few weeks, after all. I should give him some more time before dumping my feelings on him. For now, let me just focus on the fact that he's coming over.

It even works out I don't have to ask my manman for permission since she and Don are away for the weekend, celebrating their anniversary. Now, I don't have to be all alone in this house.

I straighten up the living room and, after thinking about it for a moment, make sure that my room is neat too - just in case he wants to see it.

By the time I finish putting the last of my dirty clothes in the laundry, I hear the doorbell ring. I rush downstairs to open the door for Josué and my heart breaks when I see his eyes are red. I open my arms wide, and he steps into them, scooping me up as he does so.

"I am so, so sorry, Josué."

"Thanks, Gaelle." he whispers back and then steps out of my arms. I feel colder without him. "Here, let me close the door. You're shivering." He comments as he does what he said.

"That can be easily remedied with some cuddles,." I respond teasingly.

He takes off his jacket and boots and I motion to

where he should put them. Then I go to sit on the three-seater couch in the living room and pat the open space beside me. When he sits down, I turn to face him. "Do you want to talk about it?"

He shakes his head. Hmmm. What could we do to get his mind off of the situation? Then it hits me we're actually alone.

"Do you want to not talk at all?"

He looks at me in surprise and then gives me a mischievous smile, nodding his head.

Confidently, I sit up on my knees so that our faces are at the same height and lean forward to kiss him. He kisses me back without caution, almost desperately, and I match his energy. Through this kiss, I finally express all my feelings to him.

His hand cradles my face and then goes to my hair, running his fingers through my faux locs. As he deepens the kiss, I move to sit on his lap, my hands going to the back of his neck. His hands move from my hair to my back, under my shirt. The skin to skin contact there causes a sound to erupt from me that makes him kiss me hungrier - as if he can't get enough of me. I'm unsure of how much time has passed when I feel something hard underneath me.

I'm more surprised at how good it feels against me than the fact that it's present at all.

I move against him, and his hands tug upwards at my shirt. I nod my head to him, and he pulls my shirt off. He breaks our kiss to feather my abdomen and then my chest with little kisses and I can't help but laugh. They're ticklish.

"Are you sure this is okay?" He checks in with me.

I nod my head. "Yeah, as long as you join the 'I'm

not wearing a shirt' club." I respond, my tone teasing. He laughs and removes his sweater. His body is lean but strong. Almost feeling like I need our skin to touch, I bring my chest against his, and I feel his heart skip a beat.

It's tantalizing that I have this effect on him.

I move to kiss him, but he shakes his head and pushes me back a bit. I'm surprised and stung by his rebuff. It must show on my face because he says, "I just want to look at you. You're so beautiful, Gaelle." His fingers graze the skin that my bra doesn't cover, and I sigh.

"You can't keep making sounds like that and expect me to keep a cool head."

"What if I don't want you to keep a cool head? What if I just want you to keep kissing me?"

He studies me hard for a moment. If he's looking to see if I'm sure, then he'll find that I am. I have never been more sure of anything in my life than I am at the reality that I just want to be as close to him as possible. I want my body to express the closeness that my heart already feels for him. He must see that I'm serious because he moves to kiss me again, his hands lightly roaming my body as my fingers play with the twists that his hair is in. I'm unsure of how long we stay like this when I hear my stomach rumble.

How embarrassing.

His laughter breaks our kiss. "Sounds like we need to get you something to eat."

I want to say to just ignore it, but I am actually starving. I was going to order something when Josué first called me and then forgot.

"Sounds like it. We can order in and see what will

come the fastest on Uber eats." I suggest, and he nods his head.

"Works for me."

I reach into the back pocket of my jeans and pull out my phone. It looks like the quickest place to us is Osmows. We both order super Chicken Shawarmas and then settle in to wait. I turn around so that my back is against his chest. He wraps his arms around me, his fingers stroking my stomach.

I feel heat pool in my core and am about to suggest we pick up where we left off when Josué says, "How about we answer some more of the questions?"

Disappointment hits me like a ton of bricks. Does he not feel the same attraction to me as I feel for him?

"Sure." I answer with little enthusiasm.

He guides my head to turn around and face him. "Hey, is something wrong?"

I sigh. Of course, he would notice. "I'm just disappointed, I guess. Like, you would rather answer questions than make out with me."

He looks shocked. "That's not it at all. I just know we're going to be interrupted in like 10 minutes and would rather have answering questions be subject to an interruption than us ..." He searches for the right words. "... physically connecting."

Relief washes over me.

"When you put it that way, it makes sense. Sure, let's go after the questions. We're almost done, right?"

"Right. We're on the third and final set."

"Okay, bring it! I'm ready."

"Damn, that determination is sexy as hell."

I can't help but laugh at this.

"Okay, make 3 true 'we' statements each."

"Hmm. We both share a Haitian heritage, we have complicated relationships with our moms, and we are attracted to each other." I answer after a moment.

"We both go to Bayview. We both don't have our dads in our lives, and we are eating Shawarma for dinner. Alright, next: complete this sentence: I wish I had someone with whom I could share my … grief." He pauses. "It feels like my friends aren't interested in it, and I have to be strong for my sisters and brother, so I can't bring it up with them. You're the only one that I feel like I can talk about it with."

I'm touched by his trust. "You can always share it with me. Anytime. I feel like between you and Ruthia, I can share my full self, so I'm not sure how to understand this question."

"No problem. Alright, if you were going to become a close friend with your partner, please share what would be important for him or her to know."

"I talk to myself sometimes." I say, embarrassed.

"All great geniuses do, I'm sure." The kindness in his voice makes me give him a warm smile. "I can be almost annoying with my constant photo-taking."

"I don't mind it at all."

"I'm glad because you are definitely my favourite subject."

I feel my face warm at his words.

"Up next: tell your partner what you like about them; be very honest this time, saying things you might not say to someone you've just met. I like the way you look up or off to the side when you're thinking. It's like you're taking whatever was said seriously."

"I didn't even realize I did that. Umm, I guess I like the way you touch me. It's very gentle almost…"

"Reverent?"

I look at him, surprised. "Yes, that's the word I was looking for."

"I worship your body, Gaelle, so I'm glad that you feel that way."

I am hardcore blushing now and just want to kiss him when I hear the doorbell ring.

"That's our food. I'll go get it. I'm a bit more decent than you at the moment." He says. I nod in agreement and move off of his lap so that he can get to the door.

Within a moment, he's back with the food, and we open the bag and tuck in. I can feel how thankful my body is to have some food in it after just a few bites. "How about we go to the next question?" I suggest.

"Sure." He puts down his shawarma to grab his phone and then reads off, "Share with your partner an embarrassing moment in your life."

"Oh gosh. I was like 9 and was swimming in a public pool when the top part of my swimsuit came undone, but I didn't realize it. So I emerged from the water without a top, just as a group of cute boys were walking by. So embarrassing. What about you?"

"I accidentally swore in church. In front of everybody in the youth group." I nearly choke on my food. "You're not serious!"

"I so am. I feel like I can never live that down."

"Oh, you can't."

"That's so encouraging, Gae."

His sarcasm makes me laugh. "You're welcome." I respond through giggles.

"Imma go to the next question. When did you last cry in front of another person? By yourself?"

I don't have to think hard about that one. "Oh, that would be on our date last week at Winterfest." I answer.

"Same. Okay, tell your partner something that you love about them already? I think I would say your empathy. You feel for people, Gae."

"Thanks, Josué. I love the way you find beauty in everything. I feel like that's where your photography comes from, you wanting to capture the beauty that few people see." I finish off my shawarma and then move closer to snuggle next to him on the couch. He wraps his arm around me, and I lean my head against his chest.

"I appreciate the way you see me, Gaelle. What, if anything, is too serious to be joked about? Suicide. Death is not something to joke around about."

"I feel you. My answer would be similar, but like mental health. I hate when people make jokes about having mental illnesses. Like, that's someone's real life that you're making a joke of, you know?"

"I know what you mean. It's a major pet peeve for sure. Next question: Your house, containing everything you own, catches fire. After saving your loved ones and pets, you have time to safely make a final dash to save any one item. What would it be? Why? That's easy, my camera."

"Yeah, that answer is on brand for you, BF." I say dryly, and he laughs.

"Am I so predictable?"

"Maybe let's say that you're just known. At least by me." I tilt my head up to give him a kiss on the cheek.

"I can live with that. What are you grabbing?"

"So basic, but my phone for pictures and notes." I

shrug.

"Nah, that makes sense. Of all the people in your family, whose death would you find most disturbing? Why?"

"My manman. She's the closest relative I have."

"Same here. If she died, I would be an orphan. That would suck."

"Facts."

"Okay, share about a personal problem and ask your partner's advice on how he or she might handle it. Also, ask your partner to reflect to you how you seem to feel about the problem you have chosen. Welp, I guess what to do about Madeline."

"Yep. Hmmm." I pause for a moment to think. "I think you should have another conversation with her, but this time try to see what makes her think she needs a cigarette. Is it grief? Is it boredom? You can't deal with the problem without knowing the root."

"My girlfriend is so wise." He leans down to kiss me on the forehead. "Thanks, Gae. I'll do that."

"You're welcome. As for the second part of the question..." I try to figure out how to word this and decide to stop snuggling with him so that he can see my face. "I also noticed that you seem to take a lot of responsibility for her behaviour. I know that you've felt like you've had to step into your dad's shoes. But you're not her parent, Josué, you're her big brother. You can release some of that responsibility that you're carrying."

He's silent, his eyes closed as he takes in what I said. After a few moments, I get worried. "Did I overstep, Josué?"

He opens his eyes and they're teary. "Not at all,

Gaelle. I just don't know how to let go of something that I feel like was given to me, not something that I willingly took up. You know?"

"Oh, Josué. I wish I had an answer for you, that I could take this weight from you. But, I can't. I'll help you carry it though any way I can."

"Thanks." He leans forward like he's going to kiss me, but then leans back. "Okay, last question! Whoop!"

His enthusiasm makes me chuckle.

"Let's do this!" I try to reflect his energy and now it's his time to laugh.

"Okay, if you were to die this evening with no opportunity to communicate with anyone, what would you most regret not having told someone? What haven't you told them yet? Oh. Well." He sighs and runs a hand through his hair. Is he nervous?

"Josué? You okay?"

"Yeah, I just." He closes his eyes and then opens them again, staring me right in my eyes. He looks scared, but sure of himself at the same time. "I would most regret not telling you how I feel about you."

My brain can't compute his words. "How you feel about me?"

"Yeah. I, I love you Gaelle."

It feels like time has frozen.

Am I breathing?

Is this what being in shock feels like?

"You… you what?"

"I love you." He sounds more confident this time. "You're the person I think of before falling asleep and right when I wake up. You're beautiful and kind and hilarious and smart. I want to hear your thoughts on everything. I love learning new things about you. I feel more known and cared for by you than anyone else in my life. I want to spend all my time with you, even if we're just doing homework. I picture my future, and I can't see it without you in it. I love you, Gaelle."

I don't even realize that I'm crying until he starts to wipe my tears away. I think about all the things that I shared with Ruthia, and I'm overcome by the weight of the words rising in me in response to his declaration.

"Josué Désulmé, I love you too." My voice is quiet, but I know that he's heard me because the biggest smile I've ever seen on his face is there right now.

"Yeah?"

"Yeah."

"She loves me back!" He exclaims in a loud voice, and I laugh.

"Who are you talking to, BF?"

"I don't know, maybe the universe? I feel like this is the best gift I've received, and I want to share it with everyone."

The joy on his face is adorable and makes me want to kiss him, so I do, climbing back into his lap as I do so. He kisses me back and we are like that for a while, just taking each other in, mapping our love across each other's bodies with our fingers. Eventually, I feel him become hard underneath me again and this time, I pull at his pants.

"Hold on a sec, Gae. Are you sure you want to keep going? I didn't say I love you so that I could get in your pants."

"That just makes me want to do this with you even more."

He stops my hands and makes direct eye contact with me. "Are you sure? I'm okay to go slow."

"I'm not saving myself for marriage, Josué. I've been waiting for love and now I have it with you. Yes, I'm sure. I want to move forward with you."

A smile breaks out on his face. "Same, Gaelle. Same. In that case, shall we move to your bedroom?"

"That's a great idea." I'm so glad that I cleaned it now!

I move to get off his lap to go upstairs, but he holds me tighter. "Nah, I'm pretty sure I can carry you. Just tell me where to go."

"Are you sur-eeee!" My question is cut off with a squeak as he stands up, lifting me with him.

"Positive."

We head to my bedroom and proceed with the most cherished moments of my life. It's slow and then fast and then relaxed again. At the end, we're spooning naked against each other and there's no other place I'd rather be than with the love of my life.

Chapter 10

"Good morning, hottie." I smile at Josue's sleepy voice coming through the phone. I squint my eyes to see him squinting his eyes at me.

"Good morning, BF. How long are you going to be doing these morning calls, by the way?"

"I don't know. It's the closest thing I can get to waking up with you. Now that I know what that feels like, it's hard to go a whole morning without seeing you."

"Such a sweet talker in the morning."

"Only to you, Gae. Only to you."

"At least we have school today, so it won't be long before we see each other in person." I remind him.

"You're right. I can't wait to touch you. I've learned that 24 hours away from you is too long."

I have to agree. He spent Friday night with me and then all day Saturday, too. But he had to go home Saturday night and with a group project, he had to work on that Sunday. We didn't get to see each other. It has felt long since we've been together.

"Yeah, right. Like, you will not get sick of me." I joke.

"I can't even imagine that happening. You're it for

me, Gaelle." It's the way he sidesteps my teasing into such a serious sentiment that has my heart beating all crazy.

"I feel the same way about you, Josué." We just stare at each other until my phone alarm goes off. "And that's my cue that I have to get out of the bed and get ready. "See you later."

"Love you, hottie."

I don't think I'll ever get tired of hearing that. "I love you too." I say quietly, and he smiles at me and waves before the call disconnects.

I decide on a thick wool lilac turtleneck with fleece-lined leggings. It's the last week before Christmas break and it seems like the weather got the memo that it's supposed to be cold now. I hum along to the Celine Dion Christmas album as I get ready.

When I arrive at school, I'm so excited to see Josué that I barely notice anyone else around me. Just barely. I recognize that there are whispers as I pass by, but that's been pretty normal ever since I started dating Josué.

I'm stopped in my tracks though when I get to my locker and see SLUT written in all caps on it in black ink.

I'm not even sure how to react. Who would do this? And how would they know that Josué and I had sex? I open my locker and then a few photos fall out. One is of me with my sheet covering my lower half while my upper body is fully exposed. The other is of me lying flat on my back with nothing covering me and one hand above my head as I stare off the camera. They're beautiful photos, but no one was supposed to see them.

No one except Josué.

"Gosh, you're beautiful. I love your body so much, Gaelle." Josué says to me, propped up on his left arm, as I prop myself up to stare at him, too.

"Why, thank you, my love. You've got that look on your face." I say teasingly.

"What look?" Now, his facial expression is one of confusion.

"The look you get when you want to take a photo." I explain.

"I didn't realize that I had one of those." He sounds amused and surprised all at once.

"Well, you do. And you can." Now he looks even more surprised.

"Are you serious? You'd be okay with me taking photos of you while naked?"

"Why not? I trust you. It's not like you'd show them to anyone." I say confidently.

"Thank you for your trust in me. Here, let me get back my camera. I think I left it downstairs."

The memory that was once sweet to me now turns bitter in my mind. No one was supposed to see these. I hadn't even seen them - and wasn't planning to.

What was going on?

Then, my phone rings. I glance at the screen to see that it's Ruthia. She never calls on a Monday morning. "Thia?"

"Gaelle, have you been on Facebook?"

"No, not for a few days now. You know I'm usually on Instagram. Why?"

"Sit down for this." Her voice sounds so sombre and in an instant, I know it must be related to the photos.

"Just tell me, soeur."

"Someone has posted a bunch of naked photos of you on Facebook, and they've tagged you in them. I just saw them and called you right away."

It's like someone has dumped cold water over me. "What's the name on the account?"

"John Doe. It's a burner account. Someone made it just to post these. I'm so sorry, Gaelle. Is there anything I can do?"

"You calling me and filling me in is just what I needed. I don't think there's anything else you can do at this point."

"Okay, keep me updated on the situation."

"I will, bye."

"Bye."

I stare at my phone in my left hand and the photos in my right.

Against my better judgement, I log onto my Facebook account and am inundated with notifications. First of me being tagged in a bunch of photos, then comments and reactions to the photos.

'Hawt,'

'Damn.'

'Didn't know she was a porn star in training.'

'Free porn!'

I tap away from the app when I can't read anymore. Then I go back and untag myself from the photos, but it feels like I'm too late. So many people have seen the photos already and know that it's me.

"Hottie!" I look up to see Josué coming towards me. Just before he can touch me, I flinch away. I see the hurt flicker across his face. "Gaelle, is something wrong?"

I laugh bitterly. "Of course, something's wrong. Look at these!"

It takes a moment for him to register what I'm showing up, but when I do, I can see he looks like he's going to be sick.

"How did you get those?"

"Someone planted them in my locker."

"I still don't understand."

"*Someone* posted your photos on Facebook and now tons of people have seen them and know that it's me."

"Oh my gawd, Gaelle. I had no idea." He reaches towards me, but I take a step back. "I'm so sorry. What can I do?"

"What can you do? You can take them down!"

"Take them down? You think I did this?!"

Do I think he did this? My heart is telling me no. That he loves me and would never degrade me in this way. On the other hand, my mind is reminding me they're his photos. If he didn't post them, who did?

"I don't know what I think anymore." I admit. "All I know is that they're your pictures of me that were meant to stay private and are now super public."

Then we hear a message over the PA. "Josué and Gaelle, please report to the principal's office."

We look at each other. This has to be about the pictures.

The secretary gives us both a kind smile and motions for us to head on in. We walk past her to an office with an open door. Sitting there is our principal, a small Chinese woman: Principal Chow. I've only seen her smiling at assemblies, but now she looks serious.

"Your mothers are on their way, but before they

get here. I want to see if there's anything that either of you wants to say. I'm sure you know that you're here because of the sexual pictures that were posted late last night of Gaelle, presumably by you, Josué."

"It wasn't me."

"That remains to be seen." She answers. "Gaelle, how are you feeling?"

"I feel …" I think for a moment. "Betrayed, exposed, attacked, violated. I could go on."

"All those feelings make sense. Those pictures show that there was a lot of trust between you two and now that trust has been broken."

"Exactly!" She should actually be a therapist, not a principal.

"I didn't do it. Gaelle, I would never do something like that to you. I love you."

For the first time since he's said that to me, I can't say the words back. It's not that I don't love him anymore, feelings don't go away that easily. But, like Principal Chow said, I can't trust him. How did these pictures get out? I just need an answer to that question. Was this his plan all along? String me along, tell me he loves me just to get these photos and post them online? Why would he do that to me? Why?

"Gaelle!" I see my manman burst through the office door, and I'm in her arms immediately. "Je suis désolée, ma chère." She whispers to me. I don't know if it's her presence or her speaking our heart language, but the floodgates open and I can't stop crying. "Shhh. Shhh. I'll fix this. I'll fix it all."

I nod against her and then we pull back from our embrace. During that time, Josué's mom had showed up and was talking furiously with him.

Principal Chow clears her throat. "Now that we're all here, we need to figure out what has taken place and what the consequences will be."

"I think it's quite obvious what has happened. This young man took advantage of my daughter and posted these pictures of her on social media. He should be expelled." My mom says vehemently and slams her fisted left hand on the principal's desk.

"What are your thoughts, Mrs. Désulmé?"

"I'm ashamed to call Josué my son. He should get whatever punishment is appropriate. I know his father would agree with me if he were here."

At this, I glance at Josué. He looks sombre. Those words must be killing him, and I want to comfort him. What is wrong with me? I'm the victim here! But it's hard to fight off the real love I have for him.

"Well, our school has a zero-tolerance cyberbullying policy, so expulsion is on the table. Josué, do you have anything to say for yourself?"

"I don't care what happens to me. I just don't want to lose Gaelle."

"Gaelle, do you have anything to say to that?" Principal Chow turns the table to me.

"None of this makes sense. I just want this whole situation to go away." I say, the tears returning.

"But how do you feel about me?" Josué asks me directly.

I can't look at him without feeling pain. "What I feel is irrelevant to the situation."

"How can you say that?"

"Because there are naked pictures of me online for everyone to see and you won't take responsibility for your part in that, whatever your part is!" He flinches at my words, like I've slapped him. Like, he's the victim in this situation.

Unbelievable.

This entire relationship has been unbelievable from the start. I knew that something was off. I knew it was too good to be true. But here I am, humiliated, and for what?

I'm crying again now and my manman pulls me close to her.

"What do you want, Gaelle?" She asks me.

"I just want to disappear. I never want to see Josué again." Hurt fills his eyes, but I force myself not to care.

"Is that possible?" My manman asks Principal Chow.

"Yes. Josué, unless you can prove you didn't post those photos, you are expelled. You will be transferred to another school within the school board starting right after Christmas break." Principal Chow says with a sense of finality.

The rest of the morning is a blur. Once the punishment has been meted out, I decide I can't handle being around my classmates for the week, so we pick up work from my teachers and then head home.

The whole time, I see Josué's eyes filling with hurt and, as soon as I get home, I cry myself to sleep.

Chapter 11

Manman steers clear of me for the next few hours, but around lunchtime, she pokes her head into my room.

"Ready to talk about it?"

I shake my head 'no' but she comes in anyway.

"That's okay, you don't have to. But I'm just going to be here so that you know that you're not alone." She says as she gets comfortable on my bed.

We stay silent for I'm not sure how long, but I crack. Her presence makes me want to share. I remain lying down but turn onto my side so that I'm facing her.

"I just feel so humiliated and betrayed."

"Mhmm."

"And stupid."

"Your feelings are valid, but I have to correct you a bit. You're not stupid."

"Aren't I though? I let a guy I barely knew take pictures of me while naked because I thought he loved me and I loved him back."

"I doubt that you barely knew him. It might not have been a long time, but the heart can fall pretty fast. You weren't stupid, you were trusting. Trust always has an element of risk to it. Love has a risk to it. You're giving someone your heart and trusting that they'll protect it and do good to it. If they do, it's a huge payoff. If they don't, it causes a lot of pain."

"I don't think I ever want to love someone romantically ever again, Manman. It's too painful. I don't know if the risk is worth it."

"I know how you feel, ma chère, but don't make vows like that while you're in pain. When the pain fades, you'll have to live with those promises that you made to yourself and to the Universe - and you don't want that."

I sigh. She's right. Her life is such an example of this. She could find love after what my papa did.

"Now, I have a few practical questions for you if you're up for answering them?"

"Sure, go ahead." I roll onto my stomach and prop my head up with my hands, giving her my full attention.

"How long have you been sexually active? And did you use protection?" Her face is cautious as she asks me these things.

"Just this past weekend, while you and Don were away. And, yes. We did."

At my answer, she relaxes. "Phew, good because I'm not trying to be a granmè soon." We laugh together at that statement. "Speaking of granmè, I want to remind you that yours is coming over to spend time with us over your Christmas break."

"Oh no, you won't tell her, will you?" Imagining my innocent granmè knowing about me having sex and the pictures immediately makes me feel anxious.

"I won't. Your granmè is very conservative. We'll spend the week sight-seeing Toronto as a family and going shopping. The one thing, though, that we'll all have to put up with is going to church on New Year's Eve. It's something that she always does at her Haitian church back in Montréal. She found a Haitian one here that has a service too, so we'll be going."

"I can live with that. It's not like we have any major traditions for what we do on New Year's anyway. Who knows? It might be a good time."

My mom gives me a skeptical look. "I'm glad to see that your sense of optimism is intact. Would your appetite be as well? I have some food for you downstairs."

I don't feel hungry, but I know that it's wise for me to eat. "Sure, I can eat."

"That's my pitit fi [*daughter*]." She says with a smile, and I find it in me to smile back.

I think I'm going to survive this after all.

~

The next two weeks are spent shopping, doing homework, and trying not to think about Josué.

Easier said than done.

After deactivating my social media accounts per Ruthia's and manman's counsel, I still itch to go back to the conversations that he and I shared.

I miss him.

It feels like my life has a Josué-shaped void, like I'm empty without his presence in my life.

Having granmè around is helpful though. She makes me laugh and always finds the positive in any situation that we're in; she's like a piece of home come to visit with us, and I'm so grateful for that. It reminds me of who I was before I even knew Josué existed; someone vibrant and fun and … whole.

The days fly by and it's New Year's Eve; time to go to church.

As we pull into Tabernacle de Sainteté [Holiness Tabernacle], I feel a mix of nervous excitement. What will it be like? Will I understand why Ruthia seems to enjoy church so much?

We take a while to find a parking spot because the lot is small. Don opts to park on the grass. The church building seems to be on the smaller side from the outside, but once we open the doors, I realize that it's larger than it seems.

Women who look to be about my manman's age greet us. "Akeyi, bienvenu, welcome."

"Mèsi [*thank you*]." My granmè responds joyfully. She is in her element. You would think that she's been attending this church her whole Christian life instead of being a first-time visitor. We follow her to some a few rows from the front on the left side of the sanctuary.

I glance around the room as I take off my jacket and I'm struck by how much I don't stand out. Almost everyone except Don is Black and the languages I'm hearing are a mixture of English, French and Kreyol.

It's weird to feel like I belong.

We're not waiting for very long when a woman comes on the stage with a mic in her hand.

"Bonswa tout moun! Good night everyone! Are we ready to end this year by worshiping our God? If you are, stand up! I will pray for us and then the praise team will come up."

After a beautiful prayer that alternates between Kreyol, English and French, she gives the mic to a young woman that looks to be a few years older than me. For the next better part of an hour, we sing along to different songs. I feel bad for Don that two of the three languages present are ones he can't understand, but personally, I'm having a great time. The music is upbeat and makes you want to dance. I am reminded that the praise time would always be my favourite part when going to church with granmè.

When we're invited to sit down, music plays from the speakers, and it's time for different dance performances, from little kids to teenagers - all surprisingly well done.

Then an older man comes onto the stage.

"Bonswa Legliz! Let's praise God for our night thus far! There is a spirit of excellence in this place, amèn?

"Amèn!" Several people respond.

"Now, you know that I always seek Bondye [*God*] for a word for the New Year and I was asking Him what the vision would be. He sent me to Genesis 3. Turn your Bibles there if you have one. If you don't, we have Bibles in the back of the pews, or you can be like the young people and look on your phone."

Granmè opens her Bible while Don and Manman grab one of the Bibles in front of us. I open up the app that Ruthia had told me about that I've never opened until now.

"Eve is deceived by the snake, the devil, and eats the fruit that God told her not to eat. Then, she shares it with her husband. I'll be reading verse seven. Please stand for the reading of God's Word."

Obediently, we stand up as he reads the verse. "'Then the eyes of both of them were opened, and they knew that they were naked; and they sewed fig leaves together and made themselves loin coverings.' Frè ak sè [*brothers and sisters*], the Fall was a terrible thing. We see two of its main consequences just in these verses. First off, they realized that they were naked. This is the beginning of shame. *Wont.* Oxford defines shame as: 'a painful feeling of humiliation or distress caused by the consciousness of wrong or foolish behaviour.' Brene Brown, someone who has spent years researching shame, defines shame as: 'the intensely painful feeling or experience of believing that we are flawed and therefore unworthy of love and belonging—something we've experienced, done, or failed to do makes us unworthy of connection.' Everyone here has felt shame at some point in their life."

He definitely has my attention. I have felt a lot of shame with the whole incident with the naked photos. Even though I know them being shared publicly isn't my fault, it was painful.

"Shame started there. How do I know this? Because at the end of the previous chapter, the Bib [*Bible]* says that they were naked and not ashamed. They were comfortable in their nakedness. To be naked wasn't something to be embarrassed about. But then, as soon as they eat the fruit, they realize their nakedness and try to cover it up. Shame always makes us want to hide, retreat, or withdraw. Shame seeks to isolate us that way."

That is how I felt! I just wanted to disappear. And I didn't just feel this way after the photos. I also felt this way after the move. There was this gnawing emptiness. This feeling that I wasn't loved anymore and that must be my fault.

"The fig leaves were them trying to deal with their shame by their own efforts. But fig leaves are inadequate clothing. All our efforts to cover up our shame will never be enough. We try to cover it up with money, clothes, accomplishments, relationships, but they never work. They never get rid of the feeling that we're not worthy of being loved, that there's something wrong with us. They're distractions, not solutions."

Oh my gosh, he's right. Josué was like a fig leaf in my life. He gave my life a sense of meaning again after the move. He took away some of the emptiness that I was walking around with. But he didn't solve it. If anything, with the photo situation, he made it worse!

"And legliz, make no mistake. There is something wrong with us. We, like Adam and Eve, have all sinned. We all have an inclination within us to put ourselves first, to do things our own way and not God's way. The shame we carry around is a consequence of us being sinful."

He pauses here. and I'm struck by the gravity of his words. I didn't realize that was what sin meant. I didn't realize that me putting myself first was evidence of something wrong in me.

"But God did not leave Adam and Eve in that place of shame. And he doesn't leave us there either. Let's skip ahead to verse 21. This is after God has confronted them about their sin and has shared the consequences that will come from it. Then we have this verse that I'm about to read. You may be seated while I read this one: 'The Lord God made garments of skin for Adam and his wife, and clothed them.' Ooh legliz. Let's not miss the weight and beauty of this verse. Our own efforts to deal with our shame fall short, so what does God do? Does he leave them in their shame and nakedness? No!"

"Hallelujah! He personally provides clothes for them. Instead of using plants, he uses skin - animal skin - to make their clothes. This required the animal to die; to be sacrificed. This is a foreshadowing of Jesus Christ! The perfect Son of God! The only one who never sinned, never had cause for shame. He gave his life for us. And how did he die? Crucifixion! In our portrayals of the crucifixion, Jesus has a little cloth covering his genital, but that's a lie! He was crucified naked and exposed - in complete shame. I feel that someone here needs to know that Jesus knows about the humiliation of being naked before others. He lived that too. He can relate to you, whoever you are."

Immediately, tears come to my eyes. That message was for me, I'm sure of it. Just like my photos were shared publicly, Jesus knows what it's like to be publicly humiliated like that. Jesus gets it.

"He died in shame so that we could be clothed in his righteousness, his honour, His dignity. Isaiah 61:10 says: 'I will rejoice greatly in the Lord, my soul will exult in my God; For He has clothed me with garments of salvation, He has wrapped me with a robe of righteousness, As a bridegroom decks himself with a garland, And as a bride adorns herself with her jewels.' Amèn, yon moun [*Amen, somebody*]!

"Amèn." I whisper. What beautiful words. Could this really be something I claim? Could I really be clothed with salvation and righteousness?

"Does anyone here feel naked today? Exposed? Vulnerable? Receive the invitation to be clothed with Christ. That is the word for the New Year, legliz: Clothed. This year, Bondye wants us to stop walking around in our shame and nakedness and instead be clothed with his salvation and righteousness like the Bride that He's made us to be. If you want to be clothed with Christ, to receive Him as your Lord and Saviour, then I invite you to come to the front and we will pray with you."

I don't even have to think about it. I get up immediately. I hear movement beside me and see that Manman is getting up too. We look at each other in surprise and then joy, walking to the front together. An older woman prays with us and when it's done, I feel clean all over. I feel brand new. That pesky shame is gone, and it feels like freedom and hope.

Chapter 12

6 years later

"I believe that we're here." Manman says as she turns into the driveway of the seminary. "Do you know what building you're supposed to be at?"

I reopen the email on my phone. "It just says the main building."

"Those are not the most clear directions."

"You're not wrong. But it looks like there's only one large building on the grounds, so I'm guessing that we're going there."

"Kay, let me pull up right to the entrance." She drives through the parking lot to a set of double doors.

"Merci, Manman." I move to open the door and exit the car when I feel her put a hand on my leg. I turn to her, surprised.

"Are you sure that you want to do this?"

Now, I'm even more surprised. Next to Ruthia, she's been my biggest cheerleader with going into vocational ministry.

"Yes. I'm very sure. Where's this coming from, mMnman?"

"I'm just getting a sense that something hard is

coming your way. I guess I just want to protect you. I need to trust God with you. Maybe spend time with Him today when you settle in and seek His face on whatever is coming up for me. I'll be praying too."

I am touched by her protective yet surrendered heart. She's such an example to me of what it means to be a woman of deep faith in God.

"I'll do that. Mwen renmen ou [*I love you*]." I give her a kiss on the cheek and then leave the car. She pops open the trunk for me to grab my carry-on bag that is holding my things for the next few days.

"And you have a ride back, right?"

I'm not that sure about that, but I don't want her to worry. "Yes. See you at the end of this week." I wave goodbye and she waves back before driving away.

I'm here. I'm actually here!

I decide to take a selfie at the entrance and send it to the Hawt Messies group chat, tagging Michelle. I type out a brief message telling them I've arrived at the seminary for New Staff Training.

Immediately, there are different celebratory emojis being sent into the chat. I smile at their encouragement. They've been so helpful with me this entire process of me finding a ministry that I resonated with, championing me on my summer missions trip, and discerning between medical school or joining staff.

I smile at their messages and then take a deep breath to dispel any lingering nerves I'm feeling. Then I go through the double doors and find myself in a long hallway. Maybe registration is at the end of it? We'll see.

As I walk down the hallway, I hear the sound of voices and chatter. I speed up and see the hallway widen into a foyer. There's a glass wall showing the quad outside. Up against the window wall are different tables and chairs set up. And in the middle of it all are a few people behind tables that are laden with lanyards and envelopes.

Bingo.

I walk up to the table and offer a smile. "Hi, I'm here for New Staff Training?"

"Welcome! Let's get you all set up. What is your name?" One woman, a short brunette with a kind smile, says.

"Gaelle Louissaint."

She scans a piece of paper and then finds what she's looking for. "Perfect. You're in the Augustine dorms, number 38." She grabs a key from an envelope with A38 on it. "Here's your key. Try your best not to lose it or we'll have to pay for its replacement. You'll see signage for the Augustine dorms across from the main parking lot. There's no curfew, but please refrain from having guys in your dorm or going into a guy's dorm."

"On this table," she gestures to the table to her left, "You'll find lanyards with an attached schedule for the next few days and a place to write your name. Try to wear your lanyards at all times so that we know that you're a part of our group and people can learn your name." She pauses. "I think that's everything. Do you have any questions?"

I shake my head no. What an overwhelming amount of information. Nerves rise once more.

"I know that it's a lot, but I'm excited about this journey you're on of joining staff with us. You're going to have a great few days here. I'm sure of it."

Her words calm my nerves. "Thank you …" I look down at her lanyard. "… Mandi. I appreciate your words."

"You're welcome. You're one of the first people to arrive, so feel free to relax in your dorm. Dinner is at 5, but come back a bit earlier to meet your peers."

"Okay, sounds good. Thank you." It's only 1:30, so I have tons of time.

"No problem." I smile at her and then grab a lanyard and scrawl out my name.

With that and my key, I make my way to my dorm. Once outside, I see the sign for Augustine right away and head in that direction. I wonder if they named all the dorms after influential early Christians. The dorms are less like the apartment buildings I was expecting and more like little townhouses.

I find number 38 and let myself in. I glance around for signs that anyone else is here and breathe a sigh of relief when it looks like I'm the only present. I am in need of some alone time to process where these nerves are coming from.

After doing a quick walk through of the dorm, its kitchen, dining area, living room, downstairs bedrooms and upstairs bedrooms, I choose one bedroom upstairs to settle into. Instead of unpacking my stuff, I opt to drop on the bed. Surprisingly, it's comfortable. Maybe I should take a nap. But then, I remember my mom's recommendation to spend some time with God.

That's what I should do with this alone time.

I unzip the outside pocket of my carry-on and pull out my journal and a pen. Then I settle in for some listening prayer. This practice of being still and just listening for what God might want to say to me has been so beneficial to my relationship with Him in fostering more intimacy between us.

I recite the prayer that I now have memorized. "Lord, my God, I come to you now just wanting to hear from you. I quiet my soul and remember that you are God, and I am not. In the name of Jesus Christ, I command any voice other than the true God - be it the world, my flesh, the devil or my own understanding - from speaking or interfering with this time. Come, Lord Jesus. Come, Father God. Come, Holy Spirit. Transform me into Your very likeness with Your words. I am listening to You and You alone. Amen."

After a few moments, I hear God's voice speaking to me. Not audibly, but more like thoughts that are not my own thoughts in a voice that sounds deep, like thunder or rushing water. I immediately write down the things that he says:

"Beloved Gaelle,

I love you so much. I am pleased with you, with your decision to spend time with Me and with your decision to obey Me by going into this ministry. You have chosen the path of obedience and dependence. It will not be easy, but it will be good. When difficulty arises, continue to lean on Me and trust Me. I will bring you through. I will take care of you. I will never leave you nor abandon you, so be strong and courageous!"

My eyes begin to tear up at His words to me. Then, I feel a sense to read Psalm 66. I grab my phone, open my Bible app, and swipe to the chapter. I shiver when I read verses ten through twelve: "For You have put us to the test, God; You have refined us as silver is refined. You brought us into the net; You laid an oppressive burden upon us. You made men ride over our heads;

We went through fire and through water. Yet You brought us out into a place of abundance."

I know these verses are the reason that I was led to this psalm. What God said about it not being easy echoes through my mind.

"Lord, I submit to Your refining and purifying process. I just want to be more like You. Accomplish that by whatever means You deem necessary. I will trust You, through fire and water. I will trust that You are bringing me to a place of abundance; of me experiencing the abundant life that You promised, Jesus. In Your name, amen."

After closing in prayer, I'm reminded of the song "Refiner" and pull it up on my phone, singing along with it tearfully. Whatever God has in store, I want the result enough to surrender through the process, no matter how painful it may be.

I check the time, and I'm surprised to see that it's already been almost an hour and a half since I was at the registration table. A part of me wants to just stay in my room until dinnertime, but I remind myself to not be led by my nerves. God told me to be courageous, and I'm going to listen to Him. Plus, everyone here has felt the same call to minister to students.

These are my brothers and sisters in every sense of the word.

Bolstered by my inner pep talk, I put on my lanyard, drop my key into my jeans pocket, reapply deodorant because stress sweating is a thing that was happening to me, and head towards the main building.

I re-enter the same double doors from earlier and walk down the now familiar hallway. As I reach the point right before the hallway widens into the foyer, I hear a laugh that I haven't heard in a long time and am stopped in my tracks. My mind must be coming up with things. There's no reason for him to be here. Cautiously and quietly, I enter the foyer and my eyes spot him.

Josué.

He's taller, now approaching at least 6'4. His shoulders are broader. He has a beard, which only makes him more attractive than he already is.

It feels like my brain has short-circuited.

My first coherent thought is that the past six years have been good to him. My second thought is a loud cry for help!

I back away from the foyer before Mandi can notice and potentially draw attention to me. Then, I walk down another hallway and climb the stairs I find. It leads to an auditorium. I sit in one chair and go to the Hawt Messies chat and start a video call.

Ruthia, Amy and Eleora answer. "What's up, soeur?" Ruthia asks.

"Yeah, are you okay? I know you wouldn't have called if something hadn't happened." Amy chimes in.

"Gaelle, are you crying?" Eleora asks gently. I touch my face and feel that it's wet. I nod.

"What's going on, love?" Ruthia asks.

"Josué." I manage to say quietly.

Ruthia swears and the girls react with alarm. "What or who is Josué?" Amy asks.

"Gaelle's ex-boyfriend from high school. The relationship ended badly with nude pictures of her being shared on social media." Ruthia answers angrily.

"And he's there, at New Staff Training?" Eleora clarifies.

I nod my head again.

"That means that God must've done some powerful work in this guy's life. Praise God!" I hadn't even gotten there in my thoughts yet, but Amy's right. God changed his life.

"I'm reminded of King David. He had that whole terrible issue with Bathsheba, but God calls him a man after His own heart. God has been in the business of transforming lives and forgiving sinful men when they repent for a long time. He could've done the same thing with Josué." Eleora adds.

"Preach Ellie!" Amy says enthusiastically. "Ruthia, you're uncharacteristically quiet."

"I know I should be all for God changing his life and all, but I remember when everything went down six years ago. It was terrible, y'all. Your girl was heartbroken. I'm thinking of how she can miss New Staff Training and still be obedient to God."

I laugh at this, remembering that God had told me it wouldn't be easy. I just didn't expect it to be this hard.

"Gaelle, talk to us, love." Eleora says, her voice as gentle as earlier.

"I think I'm still in shock. I know you guys are right, but I literally haven't had any contact with him since the incident and all the hard feelings from that are coming up. I know that the only way out, though, is through. I know that I'm supposed to be here, and I don't think I'll be able to avoid him for the next few days. I'll have to interact with him. I just need prayer for how to do that well."

"We gotchu." Amy says confidently. "I'll pray for you right now. Heavenly Father, we come to You now. We ask You to give Gaelle Your perspective on this situation. Help her see her ex the way You see him. Give her grace to interact with him in ways that are consistent with the fruit of the Spirit. Amen."

"Amen. Thank you, sisters. I'll keep you guys posted." I respond, giving them a shaky smile, and end the call.

Chapter 13

I avoid Josué throughout dinner and the evening session. It's only when we have to go around and introduce ourselves that I know he knows I'm here. I look everywhere but at him when my turn comes. I didn't want to see his reaction to my presence. By the time the evening session wraps up, I'm vibing with the girls in my dorm, and we decide to turn in early and get to know each other more. It's like a big missionary sleepover, and I love it.

The next morning, I grab breakfast with my dorm-mates and then we go to the room for our morning session. Last night, we talked about our values as an organization that we each need to uphold. I wonder what will be covered this morning.

After being led in a worship set by one of my dorm-mates, Sierra, and another colleague, a guy comes to the front of the room.

"Hey everyone! My name is Mark and I'm going to be sharing with you this morning. It's time to discuss everyone's favourite part of being a missionary: raising funds."

A bunch of us laugh, and Mark gives us a warm smile.

"Today, we're going to explore Biblical convictions of giving and stewardship. First, I want to start us off in 2 Corinthians 5:16-19. Let me read that for us: 'Therefore, from now on we recognize no one by the flesh; even though we have known Christ by the flesh, yet now we know Him in this way no longer. Therefore, if anyone is in Christ, this person is a new creation; the old things passed away; behold, new things have come. Now all these things are from God, who reconciled us to Himself through Christ and gave us the ministry of reconciliation, namely, that God was in Christ reconciling the world to Himself, not counting their wrongdoings against them, and He has committed to us the word of reconciliation.'"

I smile as these verses are read over us. Such a familiar scripture, yet its power has not faded with the familiarity.

"First off, we are not supposed to regard people according to the flesh. It is very easy to do this when raising funds. We can look at the flesh by considering people by their socioeconomic status, abilities, seriousness of faith, race or culture, age, and there are more categories. So then, if we're not supposed to see people using these categories, how are we supposed to regard them? Reconciled or yet to be reconciled. When we skip to verses eighteen and nineteen, we see that we have been given a ministry of reconciliation. We are reconciled to reconcile others. When we invite people to support our ministry financially, we are giving them an opportunity to participate in reconciliation. We must remember that."

I never saw this scripture that way before, but he's right! This is what we're inviting people to.

"Financial support raising is hard to do because money is a sensitive topic. Yet, let me encourage you and tell you that money is nothing but a currency. It is only useful for identifying what we value and what we will give our lives to. When we're talking about money, we're touching upon the Biblical principle of stewardship."

He's right. Money is so sensitive. Especially in my culture, we don't talk about it, and we definitely don't ask people for it!

"What is stewardship? To hold in trust for the rightful owner. Therefore, is anyone wealthy? No, because everything is God's. And all the reconciled are stewards. When we are raising support, we can say: 'I'm not here for your money, because it's not your money. Everything is God's. I'm here to see if you are a person that God wants to work through to provide.' Do you hear me, y'all? It's not theirs, and it will not be yours when they donate. It's always God's. This frees us from feeling indebted or from performance. It's not about us; it's about God and his ministry of reconciliation."

He's blowing my mind right now. I never saw money that way before, but I know what he's saying is true. It all belongs to God, not to us. It reminds me of the steward in Lord of the Rings, who was self-deceived into thinking he was the true master. Lord, let that never be me.

"This is what we're inviting people into. When we engage in raising financial support, we are engaging in discipleship. We are teaching people they are stewards and giving them an opportunity to practice their faith through generosity. People engage in giving when they see three things: clarity, competency, and compassion."

Why aren't I taking notes? I open my notes app on my phone to write the three Cs that he just shared.

"First, you must have clarity of your calling and vision. Who are you and why are you here? Your calling is the how of fulfilling your purpose. Our purpose is to worship God and share Him with others. Our calling is how we go about doing that, in the use of the talents and spiritual gifts that God has given us to meet a need in the world that God has broken your heart for. Every believer has the same purpose on this planet, but not every believer has the same calling."

I always heard those terms used interchangeably, but the distinction he's drawing makes sense.

"For example, Paul shares with the church in Galatia in Galatians chapter two verses seven through nine that he had a specific calling to share the gospel with Gentiles (non-Jews) while James, John and Peter were called to share the gospel with the Jews. We see Paul in the book of Acts do many things - assignments - but they are all under the same calling to the Gentiles. This ministry that you're raising support for is your current assignment, and one day, it may change. But your calling won't."

Now we've added assignments to the mix. I'm glad that he clarified that because it would be so disorienting if I thought this job was my calling and not an assignment. Like, what if I thought God was calling me elsewhere after 10 years? It would put me in a place of confusion about God's will for my life. Knowing that this is just an assignment though gives me freedom to change.

"I want to encourage you to nail down your

calling. If you're not sure what it is, take notes of this process I'm about to outline for you. First, choose 3-7 Scriptures that are especially meaningful to you. Then consider why God has emphasized these verses in your life. Write single words or themes that stand out to you from these passages. Then, answer the following questions: What are you passionate about? What gifts has God given you? What are your strengths? What need in the world burdens you the most? Where do you have the greatest opportunity to love others?"

I decide to take a picture of his slide with all the questions instead of racing to write them down. Work smarter, not harder.

"The next two are competency and compassion. Competency is about whether you can do the thing you just shared in your calling. Compassion is the relational element. People should know that you care about your relationship with them and the students that you're looking to reach. The truth is this: You are your biggest donor, you will give the most time, money and energy than anyone else; do you even think that you're worth it? Are your answers regarding clarity, competency and compassion enough even for yourself?" He lets the question hang in the air.

"Here's the thing. You wouldn't be in this room if they weren't. Now, it's about you being able to communicate it well enough and watch God provide for you. Let me pray for you, brothers and sisters." He bows his head, and we all follow suit. "Gracious God, Generous God. All we have is Yours. Let us live in and live out the reality of this truth. Be with these new missionaries. Help them have clarity on their calling, be competent in You and show Your compassion to all they meet. Provide for each one what they need in their support raising process. We ask this in Jesus' name, amen."

After he prays, he leaves the front of the room, and we all clap for him. I make a mental note to talk to him after the morning session is done. Mandi comes to the front of the room.

"What a wonderful talk for us this morning," she says. "Now, we want to give you time to apply the process that he shared. You're going to have the rest of the morning to spend time with the Lord and nail down your calling. Leave the room if you want. You can go to your dorms or find a space around this building. The time is yours."

Bless. I'm glad that they're giving us time for this. I decide to go to an armchair that I'd seen earlier on my way to this room from the cafeteria this morning. Thankfully, no one else is around.

I pull out my phone and go back to the slide that I'd taken a picture of. The first step is to think of at least three verses that are meaningful to me. Romans 10:13-15 comes to mind. Then, the story of the Good Samaritan from Luke 10. What else? Oh, Genesis 3:21; that's the verse that led to me becoming a Christian after all.

I glance back down at my phone for the next step: writing themes from the passages. Hmm. The Romans one has the theme of sharing the gospel with those who have no one to share it with them. The Good Samaritan is a picture of mercy and showing holistic love for your neighbour. Genesis 3 has God taking care of Adam and Eve's need for clothing through sacrifice. Altogether, what emerges is God taking of my needs, empowering me to take care of others through proclamation and compassionate care. Or, even, God models what care looks like, and I'm just seeking to follow Him in that.

Now it's time to answer the questions he gave. What am I passionate about? I'm passionate about people hearing the gospel. Everyone should have the opportunity to respond to God's invitation of relationship. Ever since I first came to know Jesus, I've been passionate about sharing Him with the people around me. Getting involved with Students for Jesus only nurtured this passion and equipped me to share well.

What gifts has God given me? Well, I'm bilingual, empathetic, encouraging and able to see how people need the gospel intuitively upon meeting them. Those would be the same as my strengths, I think. What need in the world burdens me the most? The unreached. It is mind-blowing to me, in the most negative way possible, that people still don't have access to the gospel in their lifetime. Where do I have the greatest opportunity to love others? Well, by working with international students, my chosen role, I am working with the unreached right at home in a way that's strategic and holistic.

Okay, so putting all of that together, what is my calling? Working with international students is my current assignment, but it's not my whole calling. My calling would be to the unreached. After re-reading all my notes multiple times, I know what to write.

My calling is to embody God's holistic (practical and salvific) care towards the unreached.

I look down at the words I've just written, and they fill me with a sense of zeal and rightness. This is why

I'm here on this earth, to embody who God is and has been to me, to others, specifically the unreached.

I'm about to bow my head and pray when a shadow falls over me. I look up and all the good feelings I had vanish.

It's Josué.

Chapter 14

"I hope I'm not interrupting." He runs his hand through his hair. "It's just that it's lunchtime, and I thought it might be a good time as any for us to talk."

His voice is different. Deeper. Richer. I heard it last night, but I was doing everything in my power to not pay attention. Now, though, it's unavoidable.

He's unavoidable.

I turn over my options. The right thing to do is hear him out. I know that. Still, a part of me just wants to run and hide. The scared part of me. And God and I had a talk last year about how I need to stop being led by fear, but by trust in Him.

The trusting God thing to do would be talking with Josué.

I sigh and motion to the other armchair beside me. "Sure, let's talk."

He releases a breath that I didn't even realize he'd been holding and nods, sitting in the chair. "Well, to be honest, I had prepared for you to refuse to talk to me, so I hadn't planned what I was going to say beyond asking to talk."

I can't help but chuckle at this. Six years later, and he still knows me so well. "Well, take your time. I'll just be starving as I wait." I joke, making him crack a smile.

Why does his smile have to be so devastating?

Then he takes something out of the satchel that he's wearing. "I brought one of the chicken wraps from the cafeteria. It was between that and tuna, and I know how you feel about fish. At least, I did? Maybe you like fish now - sorry for assuming. I shouldn't ha-"

"It's okay." I cut his rambling short. "You made the right choice. Thank you."

There's that smile again.

I take the offered wrap, and as I do, our fingers graze each other. It's the lightest contact, but it sets my arm ablaze.

I can't believe that he still has this effect on me.

He clears his throat. "So, the first thing that needs to happen is that you need to read this," Josué says, and then hands me his phone.

It takes a moment for me to realize what I'm looking at, but when I do, there's an instant double-take. His phone is showing a message from a girl named Kaitlin that used to be his friend in high school. It reads:

> OMG. Jo. I'm so so so sorry. I didn't know that they would expel you for the photos. I'm the one who posted them. When I was over for that Business project that we were working on, I was on your computer and came across the photos. I was creeping to see what new photos you'd taken since I'm, like, obsessed with your talent. But then, I saw the photos of gaelle and got sooo jealous. So, I sent them off to myself and you can put the rest together. I swear, if I'd known

that you would get in so much trouble, I wouldn't have done it. I would never want to do anything to hurt you. I'm going to turn myself in. You don't deserve to be punished for my mistake. I hope you can forgive me someday.

I nearly drop his phone in shock at the confession. "I don't understand."

"The message wasn't clear?" He looks confused.

"No, I get her confession. I just don't understand how I'm just hearing about this now. You never came back to school. She was never expelled. The math isn't mathing."

"Ahh. Well, I chose to not go back. They cleared it from my record and just logged me changing schools as a transfer student. As for Kaitlin, I'm pretty sure her dad paid someone off to keep it hush and keep her in school."

I shake my head. "That's crazy. White people can get away with almost anything."

"Or rich people."

"And there's a lot of overlap between those two categories."

"Sorry, you're sounding a bit too woke right now. I'm going to have to rescind your Christianity membership card," he says, making his voice sound official.

"Pretty sure man can't take that away and Jesus said he wouldn't give up any of his sheep, so… tough toughies for you."

At this, he bursts into laughter, and I follow suit. The laughter clears the air of any residual tension or awkwardness that remained.

"One last question about this: why didn't you tell

me?" My question hangs in the air as Josué stares at me. It becomes too much for me to bear, and I break eye contact first. Why did it feel like he was staring straight into my heart?

"You wanted to put it all behind you, including any association with me. I wanted to respect that. I'm sharing now though because we're going to be seeing a lot of each other and I didn't want you to keep hating me." His voice is sad now, all traces of humour forgotten.

"I've never hated you, Josué." I see the surprise on his face at these words. "But thank you for the distance and for telling me now." He nods his head and then works on his own wrap, reminding me that mine is still untouched in my lap.

For a few moments, we share the same space and eat. It's a comfortable silence, one that bears witness to the familiarity we once shared.

"So, I'm curious. When and how did you become a Christian and join SFJ?"

This marks the first time I've seen a full smile on his face in this interaction, and I feel my heart forget how to work.

"I was wondering the same things about you!"

"But I asked you first." I tease, and he laughs.

"Fair enough, but I expect you to share next. Deal?"

"Deal." I nod my head for extra measure.

"Okay, well. I grew up in the church, you know this. But nothing ever clicked for me; it was just something that my family did. But in the summer between the end of grade 12 and the beginning of my undergrad, I went on a missions trip with my family's church to this Indigenous camp."

"You went on a missions trip even though you wouldn't have called yourself a Christian?"

"Oh no, I would've said that I was a Christian. But I know now that I wasn't. I was barely even going through the motions of Christianity. Still, I was encouraged to go on the missions trip, so I went. And then on the trip, there was a moment when I encountered the power of God. So, I had a friend, Kyle, who was in so much physical pain. Like writhing in pain. When I entered the room, I fell on my knees because there was such a spiritual heaviness in the room. And then I started praying, but like praying scriptures, I didn't even remember reading before - word for word. I remember trembling and crying because I was literally feeling God's power as He spoke through me. And in that moment, I knew God was real, and He wanted a genuine relationship with me. All the things that I heard about Jesus and the cross and sin, it all made sense. A few weeks later, I was baptized."

I get chills as I hear him recount his testimony. How powerful!

"For joining SFJ, well, that's a lot less of a dramatic story. I was on campus, saw a poster advertising a BBQ and wanted free food. When I got to the BBQ, I realized it was a Christian club and was excited to meet other people who believed in Jesus. I ended up joining one of the Bible studies and grew so much in my faith. Then, we had a week of evangelism on campus, and I grew in learning how to share my faith. I was sold on that, and the rest is history. Went on a few missions trips to Nepal and India, then I did a one-year internship in India right after graduating. I'm trying a domestic internship to help discern whether I should be here or go back to India long-term. I'll be working with international students in Brampton at Sheridan and Algoma, since that's where a lot of South Asian students go."

Oh wow, we're both working with international students! That's crazy.

"And I've been talking for a while. I should shut up, eh? That's it. I'm going to start eating so that you can talk."

I chuckle as he takes a big bite of his wrap.

"You're not monopolising the conversation, okay? I've been enjoying listening to you and hearing about God's work in your life! It's amazing."

"Yeah, he's good."

"Tout le temps [*all the time*]!" I say automatically.

"Et tout le temps…" He follows up.

"Il est bon [*He is good*]!" I finish for him.

We smile at each other and then he gestures towards me. "Your turn now, Gaelle."

So, I share with him how I came to faith after the whole nude photos incident. He shakes his head in wonder at the timing. As I talk about me seeing an SFJ booth at a club fair and then signing up for a Bible study, he smiles at the similarity between our stories. Like him, I grew a lot in learning how to communicate my faith with others. Unlike him, I only went on one missions trip and that was a local one serving international students. That's when I felt God leading me to try an internship with SFJ upon graduation. When I finish sharing, Josué seems enthralled.

"I would love to pick your brain on International students ministry sometime since this will be my first time doing it."

"No probs, happy to help! I'm so glad that God is raising up more people to serve international students. They're such a neglected part of our society, especially by the church. But let me not get up on my soapbox about it."

"I wouldn't mind hearing your thoughts on it. Do you feel called to international students, or do you feel like it's just your current assignment?"

"That's a great question! I had just finished up my calling when you walked up to me. I feel called to the unreached. Right now, that looks like international students, but that could change."

"You're kidding. The unreached was an obvious part of my call, too! My heart just breaks that someone could go their whole lives without hearing the gospel. In India, I was the first Christian that a lot of my friends had met."

"Fam! You are speaking my heart language!" I clap my hands for emphasis. As I do, my watch screen comes on and I realize the time. "Oh shoot! Session starts in a few minutes!" I gather my Bible, journal, and pen.

"Oh man, I'm glad that you booked that because I wouldn't have even guessed that time would've flown that quickly." He grabs our empty wrappers and tosses them in the nearby garbage.

"Right? I could talk about these things forever." I get up and wait for him to put on his satchel.

"Same." We exchange smiles again, and I get sort of lost in it; the way his eyes are alit with joy, the way his beard hides the dimples I know are there. The way it feels to be in sync with him. I don't know how long we stay just staring at each other, but then we hear footsteps and are jolted back into reality.

"We should get going, eh?"

He nods and we head back towards the main session room. How I went from avoiding him to losing track of time talking to him is not lost on me, but I push any thoughts of romantic feelings away. He's my brother in Christ, and that's better than I could've ever imagined.

It's enough.

Chapter 15

It's my first fundraising appointment, and my nerves are through the roof. At New Staff Training last week, I was filled with so much vision for this process and equipped with all the practical things I needed to do it. I wish I could've had this appointment after tomorrow, when I'll be seeing everyone again virtually for the first of our weekly new staff training calls. It would be so helpful to share this appointment with them and have them pray for me.

I'm about to check my phone again to make sure I gave her the right place and time when I see Fabienne come through the entrance. I take a deep breath and wave to get her attention. She sees me and walks over to the booth where I'm sitting. I stand up to greet her and give her a quick hug. I shouldn't even be this nervous. Fab and I have a good relationship. She used to be one of my youth leaders and has now become a friend, the decade between us like nothing now. Even if she says no, this will still be a good time.

"Bonjou [*hello*], feel free to sit, and I can grab us something. What would you like?"

"I'll take a small coffee, black." She answers as she sits down.

"Okay, no problem. Be right back."

As I wait in line and pick up our drinks, I silently pray to God for wisdom in my words and courage to do the ask. When I return to the table, she puts down her phone and smiles at me. I smile back, nervously.

"Here's your coffee."

"Thank you. How have you been?"

"Hmm. I've been okay. You?"

"I'm doing pretty well."

Gosh, this is awkward. When did I become incapable of having a normal conversation?

"Hey, so you mentioned you wanted to meet to discuss this new endeavour you're on or something like that?"

"Yes! So, during my time in university, I became involved with a student ministry on my campus called Students for Jesus, or SFJ, as we call it. I grew a lot through God's work in this ministry. I learned more about my faith and how to share it with other people. I ended up going on a local mission trip with them to Guelph to work alongside international students. It was an incredible time, and I knew coming out of it that I wanted to do that after graduation. That's what I wanted to talk with you about."

"That's cool! What did you do in Guelph?"

"We partnered with different churches that ran socials for Christians to meet international students and then from those connections, we built friendships and got to share the gospel in those friendships."

"And you'll be doing the same thing now?"

"Similar, but at U of T. I'll be working with international students. I'm running a weekly French language learning time and a weekly gathering for international students to learn more about Canadian culture. I'll also be mentoring Christian international students that I meet and leaving plenty of room in my schedule to meet with non-Christian students and build friendships."

"That sounds great!"

"Thank you!" Here comes the hard part. "So, for me to do this full time, I depend on God to provide financial support since I'm not paid by the ministry, as we're a nonprofit organization. I'm trusting God to raise up 57 people who support me financially at different levels on a monthly basis. And I'm wondering if you might be one of them."

A moment of silence while she looks thoughtful, then she gives me a warm smile. "Thank you for thinking of me. I would like to do this. What are the different levels that you're thinking of?"

I breathe a sigh of relief. "3 people at 200, 9 people at 100, 12 people at 75, 15 people at 50 and 18 people at 25. But these numbers are just suggestions. You can give whatever amount you'd like." I rush to add when she's silent for a moment.

"I think I can be one of the $75 a month people. How do I go about giving?"

Oh my gosh, thank you Jesus! "I have a donation page that you can give to with your credit or debit card. You can also call or mail a cheque if those options feel more comfortable for you."

"Credit card works for me. Just send me the link, and I'll aim to set this up asap. Is that alright?"

Is that alright? It's perfect! "That's great! Thank you so much. You are the very first person I've asked. Thank you for making it such a wonderful experience for me!"

She moves her hand to right above her heart. "Oh wow, now I'm even more honoured. I'll pray that God raises up the other 56 people."

Her bringing up prayer reminds me of the other ask. "Thank you. I'll also start sending out a monthly email newsletter with stories from the work and prayer requests. Would you like to be added to that?"

"Yeah, that sounds great. I would love to be praying for you."

I clap my hands in joy. "Yay! I'll send you both the link to donate and the link to sign up for the newsletter after we're done meeting. Is there any way I can pray for you?"

I take a sip of my hot chocolate while she thinks.

"Prayer for contentment and holiness as I navigate singleness would be great. I'm struggling. I thought I would be married with kids by now and here I am now with neither."

My heart pangs at the sadness in her voice. "I can only imagine how hard it's been to be waiting so long to meet your person. If it's any help, I have a close friend in her late thirties who just got married less than six months ago. She never thought that it would happen for her, and it did."

"That's encouraging to hear. It's hard to have hope sometimes. And then..." she begins to tear up, so I reach across the table to hold her hands. "Sometimes, just looking for that satisfaction, I watch pornography. I know I shouldn't, but it feels like I can't help it. I'm just so lonely, and it helps me feel better. But then worse when I realize that I've sinned against God."

This is unbelievable! I'm stunned. Fab? Watching

porn? And she's telling me this in a Tim Hortons? I make compassionate sounds as I recover from the shock of not just what she shared but the vulnerability she's displayed in sharing it with me. Then, I remember something that one of the staff at training had said: raising financial support is an opportunity to minister to the church.

I'm feeling that right now.

"I'm honoured by your willingness to share this with me. Would it be okay if I prayed for you right now?" Fab nods and then bows her head. "Heavenly Father, Bondye, we love You. Thank You for this time to meet together and talk about what You are doing. Thank You for Your daughter and her willingness to be part of Your ministry to international students through supporting me financially. Bless her for her generosity. Senyè, we pray You would rid her of using porn to medicate her loneliness. Instead, would she find all connection and satisfaction in Your presence? We pray all this in Jesus' name, amèn."

"Amèn. Thank you, Gae."

"You're welcome, Fab." We smile at each other, and I get up to give her a hug. This went so much better than I would've thought.

God is at work.

Chapter 16

"Last week, we spent some time talking about who the Spirit is. Can anyone remember what we learned about Him?" Victoria, our new staff trainer, asks the five of us new staff who are on the call. It's our second time meeting, and I'm amped. Last week was fun and powerful.

Annie answers, "The Holy Spirit is God, The Holy Spirit is a Person and The Holy Spirit is God's Presence within us."

"That's right. Now, we're going to talk about how we walk with the Spirit in our everyday lives. This is a three-step process: recognize, remember, and respond. First, we'll talk about recognising the Spirit's work in our lives. Now, we are starting with the belief that the Holy Spirit is active in our lives and the world. He indwells us as God's presence, working through us for God's glory. However, many Christians experience His work without ever knowing that it is Him. Do you think it's a problem if the Holy Spirit is working in our lives, but we don't recognize it? Why or why not?"

We're silent for a moment and then, Josué responds. "Yes, it's a problem because then we're not giving God the glory that He deserves in our lives."

"Yep. You're right. Anyone else want to add to that?"

"We can also get discouraged because we don't think God is working in us at all." I respond after a moment.

"That's very true. So, let's go into the six ways we can experience the Spirit's work in us. The acronym I want you to remember is RECALL: relationship, effectiveness, conviction, awareness, leadership, and life. Now, let's be clear that this is not an exhaustive list of how the Spirit works. It's a snapshot. We have divided his work into these categories to help us understand the effects of His work in our lives, but He is not limited to these categories. We have also done it this way so that you can teach this to the Christian students that you minister to. Also, keep in mind that these categories can and do overlap with each other, as you can see from these circles on your screen. Now, I don't want to talk your ears off. How about we each read a section since there are six of us?" We all nod our heads. "Great. Josué, how about you start it off? Then, Annie, Timothy, Gaelle, Robby and I'll close us off. Sound good?"

"Sounds good. First off, we have relationship: 'This category speaks of how the Spirit mediates, provides proof of, and helps us experience the new relationship we have as children of God. We have included the idea of assurance in this category since in Scripture, the two are tied together.'" Josué reads.

"Effectiveness describes how the Holy Spirit empowers our gifts and actions for effective use in His kingdom purposes - whether in dramatic or gradual ways. It also describes the fruit that God bears in our lives, which makes the actions that we do reflect the God who is at work in us," Sierra continues.

"This may be one of the clearest acts of the Spirit that we experience. Conviction is awareness of areas where I'm living out of step with God's design, the Gospel, or the new person who God has called me to be," Tim reads.

I pick up where he leaves off. "'The Spirit points us to and reminds us of His presence with us. He is the one who helps us recognize His work in our lives. He helps us to know who God is and what He is doing. Our ability to partner with the Spirit hinges on the Spirit's work of giving us awareness.' Does this mean that us recognising His work is a way that He's at work?" I clarify.

"That's exactly it. Thanks for asking." Victoria answers. "Alright, Robby, you can read off leadership."

He nods his head. "The Spirit leads, guides, and helps us. For example, when we don't know what to pray for, He intercedes for us, or He testifies, speaks and counsels us."

"Great. And last, but not least, we have life. This category refers to the type of life we experience as a part of God's family. The Biblical words used in this category are freedom, satisfaction, renewal. So, when we recognize the Spirit working in us in any of these ways, we can then respond by agreeing with Him. The other response is to ignore His person, work, and voice in our lives. We can do this by claiming it to be our own work, circumstances or character, or more passively, by not listening. When might have you ignored the work of the Spirit in your life?"

"When He's convicted me of something sinful and

I keep doing it, anyway. That's a way that I've ignored Him before." Robby responds.

I nod in agreement. Been there, done that.

"Exactly, that's a good example. Thank you for sharing that with us. We want to be people who agree with the Spirit. Then we move onto the next step, which is to remember the gospel. Often, we think of the gospel as something that non-Christians need to know. Why is a growing love for the Gospel and Christ's work important for the Christian?"

"Because we are prone to wander and forget the beauty and power of it if left to our own devices. But when we remember its beauty and power, we bear more good fruit." I answer after taking a moment to think.

"Yes! Now, please note that there are many ways to remember the gospel, as we're sure you can imagine, because the breadth and the depth of the gospel are so wide and deep. We're going to go over one way that we can remember the gospel by answering different reflective questions. Tim, can you read those for us?"

"Sure, 'What is true of God? What is true of my old self/the old me? What has Christ done? How is He the hero of this story? What is my new identity in Christ or true of the new me in Christ?'"

"Thank you for reading that for us, Tim. Now we can either choose to trust in the gospel or trust in someone/something else. Trusting in the Gospel is consciously following the Spirit so that we don't just know, but believe and reorient our lives around the Gospel truths of who we are, whose we are, and the story we're in. If you're not trusting Jesus, who are you trusting? What story do you find yourself in? What do you have your hope in?"

"Okay, you better preach, Victoria!" Josué says, and we all laugh.

"Thanks, Jo. Now, I want to give us a few minutes to consider whether you are trusting in Jesus or someone/something else. Ask yourself: 'Is there anything that I think might be really good news (can save me or give me redemption), rather than Jesus?' I'll bring us back in about five minutes."

I knew this week's training would be good, but I didn't expect it to come for me like this. I guess it's easy for me to trust in my ability to do things rather than in God's ability to do things.

"Our final step is to respond to the leading of the Spirit through obedience. This can either look like starting a kingdom activity or stopping an activity. Something that's important to remember is that partial obedience or delayed obedience is still disobedience. When God tells us to do something, we obey in the timing that He's given us. Anything else is unacceptable and unworthy of His lordship in our lives. Now, I'll split you off into pairs and you can answer the following questions together: considering the work of the Spirit in your life, are there any activities that God is asking you to start? Are there any activities the Spirit is leading you to stop? Then we'll come back together, and I'll pray for us."

I wait to discover my partner and am happily surprised that it's Josué.

"Hey Gae! How has this training landed on you so far?" I feel my face warm at the casual use of my nickname. It brings back so many memories.

"It's been powerful. I didn't realize how much I'm prone to trusting in myself instead of Jesus before this training you. You?"

"Same! I can definitely recognize the Spirit at work in convicting me of the ways that I lean on my own understanding rather than just focusing on fearing Him. You know?"

"Yes! Like, one way that I know I do that is by researching a ton before deciding. I know that a part of that is me being prudent, but another part of that is me trying to figure everything out myself so that the future is less scary. I think that's one activity that I'm going to stop."

"Hmm. That's good, Gae. I'm thinking that I may need to pray more. Like, when I'm tempted to just do something, to pause and seek Him first. It's difficult because I know God still speaks, but I struggle to hear Him."

"Oooh. I can send you a process I go through to engage in listening prayer if that would be helpful?"

He looks pleasantly surprised. "That would be great! I didn't even know it was an actual thing."

"Yeah, I took part in Transformational prayer on my mission's trip and learned about listening prayer there. The facilitator recommended a book to me that outlines a way to go about engaging in it, and I've made it a consistent part of my time with God. There's so much intimacy to bc had with Him."

"I love that. I definitely want more intimacy in my relationship with God."

I'm about to respond to that when a countdown pops up on the screen. "It looks like we're about to be booted back into the main room. I'll send you the process after this call. Do you still use your IG?"

"Yep, so that works. Thanks again. It was great

talking with you!"

We wave at each other as the timer hits zero, and we're brought back into the main room with everyone else.

"I hope that the discussions you guys had were fruitful. Let me pray for us and then you can all get back to the super fun process of fundraising." We chuckle at this and then bow our heads. "Oh, Holy Spirit. We want to partner with You. Help us recognize how You're at work in our lives. Help us remember and trust the gospel. Help us follow You into whatever You've called us to next. We want to give You glory. Amen."

"Amen." I whisper, my heart feeling full of love for God and gratitude for this time.

Chapter 17

I pull into the parking lot, excitement winning out over my nerves. On the one hand, I'm nervous about going to a social for a different church's young adults. On the other hand, I'm going to be seeing a few of my Hawt Messies girl friends in person, which doesn't happen often.

When I walk into the bowling alley, I can't help but think of the last time I went bowling, which was with Josué years ago. I may or may not have been avoiding it because of the memories being so painful. Now that things are resolved, I'm curious to see if I'm still as bad as before.

"Gaelle!" I turn to see who called my name and see Eleora bounding towards me. "I'm so happy to see you!" she says as she gives me such a big hug that I almost fall over.

"It's good to see you too, love." I'm glad that she's back from school in BC.

"You're a size 9, right?"

"I am. Did you already pay for shoes?"

"Maybe?" her voice is part cautious, part playful.

"Well, that's unexpected, but thank you. I appreciate it."

She looks relieved. "You're welcome. Let me bring you over to our lane. Amy and Cass are with us."

"Sweet. I'm excited to see them."

When we get to the lane, there's a flurry of hugs when I see other girls.

"I'm always shook by how tall you are in real life." Amy comments, the shortest in our group, making me laugh.

"Legit, you could be a model, Gae." Eleora adds, just an inch taller than her.

"She is. Or, at least she was." A voice says behind me. I turn around to see Josué with a small smile on his face.

"Hey, what are you doing here?"

"I'm just started visiting this church and saw that they were having a social for young adults. You still live in Richmond Hill, though, right? What are you doing here?"

"I have friends who go to Agape and figured I'd drop by. Let me introduce them. Josué, this is Amy, Cass and Eleora. Sisters, this is Josué."

"You can call me Jo." He adds and extends his hand. They each shake it. "Well, I think my turn will be coming up soon. Chat with you guys later?"

They nod and smile at him while he walks away. Once he returns to his lane, a few lanes away from us, they immediately pull me into their fold.

"That's Josué? Girl, he's fine!" Amy whisper-shouts.

"And what's with your vibe? Am I catching a whiff of something happening?" Cass adds.

"We need an update. You haven't sent one since the SOS call." Eleora says gently.

"Oh wow. I love you guys. It turns out it was all just a misunderstanding. We're friends now. And yeah, he's aged well."

"Understatement of the century." Amy deadpans and we all dissolve into giggles.

"Okay, shall we bowl?"

"Sure, let's do it!" I answer Cass with some enthusiasm.

"Does your energy mean that you're good at this? Because, full disclosure, I suck at bowling."

"RT," Amy commiserates.

"I'm not that good either, so let's see how this goes." I assure them.

Spoiler alert: it goes badly. We barely hit 50 points by the end of our first game, but we're laughing so much at our inability to bowl that it doesn't matter.

"Lord knows, I needed this time to just be with my girls." Cass says.

"Facts. I wish Mich and Ruthia could be here." Amy chimes in.

"I know, right? But we get it. Mich's pregnancy is kicking her butt, and Ruthia has Dielle to navigate."

"Exactly, but what's up, Cass? You said that you needed this time?"

"Well, Dan and I are navigating a stupid fight, and I'm just frustrated. Partly at him and partly at myself for how I handled it."

"That sucks. But it shows that the Holy Spirit is at work in you, and that you're not happy with your own sin." I point out.

"You know, I didn't see it that way before. That makes me feel better."

"Happy to help."

"In moments like these, I'm happy to be single." Amy comments.

"Anyone on the horizon?" Eleora asks.

"Nope, no one. I think I may be called to singleness. Like, it's not that I don't find guys attractive. I don't think that I'm asexual or aromantic. I just don't feel interested in being in a romantic relationship. Does that make sense?"

"I think it's your lived experience, and that's what matters," Cass says firmly.

"Thanks, sis. How's everyone else doing?"

"Chadwick and I are good. He's in one of the other lanes. He knew I just wanted some time with you guys. We're trying to figure out timeline things, like if and when we should get married." Eleora shares.

"Oh my gosh. How do you even feel about that?" Amy asks.

"Both peaceful and wondering if I'm crazy? Like, I know we're only 20 and that's super young. But I also can't imagine being with anyone else."

"Do you think you'd get married before finishing your undergrad?" I ask.

"Honestly, we are considering it. Like maybe in the summer before our final year. In some ways, we would save more money. It's something that I'm supposed to broach with my dad and grandmothers now that I'm back, to see if they would be supportive, both emotionally and financially."

"Those sound like awkward conversations." Cass comments.

"Yeah, I'm not looking forward to it. I wish there was a blog with some sort of template for how to go about it all."

"Well, we can pray for that. And I would be happy to role play with you so that you can practice approaching the conversation."

Eleora tears up at Amy's words. "Thanks Ames. I appreciate that more than my words can say."

"We gotchu, fam!" I give her a tight side hug to punctuate my words, and she leans into me with a sigh.

"Thank you. You guys are my sisters. Like, Maryliz is still one of the closest friends but because she doesn't believe in Jesus yet, it's harder to talk about some of this stuff with her, and we've drifted apart a bit with the added factor of doing school away from each other. I just really love you guys."

"We love you too!" Cass exclaims and hugs Eleora from her other side.

"Uh, am I interrupting something?" We look up to see Chad coming towards us.

"Just feeling loved." Eleora answers.

"Good, because you are." They exchange a look filled with so much love that I feel my heart ache. "We were thinking of heading to Chuck's for some food if y'all are down."

"I could eat," Amy answers, and I nod with the other girls.

"Cool! We're going to the one on Queen. You guys are good for rides?" He asks us.

"I drove here, and I have enough room for all of us." I answer.

"Sweet. Amy and I bussed, so we would appreciate the ride." Cass responds.

"I came with Chad, but I think I'll drive over with you ladies."

"Sounds good, babe. I'll see you there," Chad says

with a wave.

"I love how he wasn't bent out of shape about you spending more time with us than with him. That's a very secure man that you have there."

"Yeah, I'm blessed with him. Let's return our shoes and get going?"

"Bet," Amy answers and we follow Eleora's suggestion.

It's a fun drive to the restaurant and when we get there, we decide to be with the larger group rather than sit off to the side by ourselves. I don't want to hog them from their own church's social, after all. Conversation revolves around what everyone's planning on ordering, but then it devolves into a discussion on theology.

"But, if God chooses us to be His people, how does our free will play a role?" a girl whose name I don't know says, her voice frustrated.

"Well, it's not like we don't have free will anymore. More like, when God reveals his goodness to someone, you wouldn't want to say no to him because he's that good," Josué responds.

"So, God doesn't reveal himself to everyone?"

An awkward silence ensues. "I think there's always going to be an uncomfortable reality that not everyone is going to be saved. The thing we have to ask is if it's because our God can be refused or because God didn't choose to save them. I think I would rather lean more on the sovereignty of God than on the free will of man. But that's just me. While it's important to know what you believe about this, it doesn't change your salvation." I end up answering when it seems like no one else will.

"Thanks, that answer is helpful. What's your name,

again? I feel like we haven't met yet, and you just helped me a ton."

"Oh." Now I'm embarrassed. "I'm Gaelle. I'm just visiting y'all since I have a few friends who go here." I give the group a wave and am warmly welcomed.

"Well, Gaelle. My name is Gideon, and I agree with you, mostly. I would just say that it affects the church you choose to go to and the ways the church practice certain things." A South Asian guy says to me.

"We all know what it's like to be at a church that has you say a salvation prayer every Sunday because they don't seem assured of their salvation." Another Black guy chimes in and most people in the group laugh, but I'm not one of them.

"Or there's a bunch of distraction because people are just speaking in tongues all over the place." The way they're talking about other churches is making me feel uncomfy.

"With no interpretation." Gideon shakes his head. "These churches will make absolutely any excuse to keep doing it, too. No matter how much you challenge that."

"No wonder most are prosperity gospel churches in the making. There's just no listening to sound doctrine. I'm so glad that I'm not there anymore and found Agape."

A bunch of "sames" echo throughout the table.

"Hey guys, we need to remember that it's members of the family that you're bashing right now. And I'm sure Agape isn't perfect." Josué butts in.

"Oh, for sure, not perfect, but definitely better." Gideon responds.

"Better in what way? A lot of the churches you're

talking about are charismatic/Pentecostal churches. And probably ethnic churches too, right? Those are the ones you were raised in?"

Gideon and the Black guy nod their heads. So do some of the other people around the table.

"Well, I'm sure there are good things there that you're missing. Ethnic churches lean on scripture memorisation and there's an understanding of submitting to church leadership." Josué says.

"Not to mention, the musical worship is lit. We also do fellowship well, staying long after the service is done to talk with each other." I add.

"Those things are true, but the bad outweighs the good. Often there's a huge focus on behaviour instead of gospel heart change. Hypocrisy is rampant. People aren't taught to read the Bible for themselves, the preaching is often good advice. I could go on." Gideon responds.

"You're acting as if multi-ethnic churches don't also have their downsides. They can be silent on issues of injustice. They can often reflect White Christian culture even as there are Brown and Black congregants. Prayer meetings aren't well attended, and people can be consumerist, putting all their stock in a Sunday morning service and what they're getting from it," Josué rebuts.

The table is silent as his words land.

"That's fair. If we can't take the heat, we shouldn't be all up in other people's kitchens," the Black guy says.

"We're not saying that Agape isn't a wonderful church. It is. You have loving pastors, and people are growing here. But it's possible to love your church without speaking badly about others." I try to say this gently and, thankfully, people look a bit chagrined.

"You're right. We need to think about how we're speaking about our extended family. I respect the rebuke," Gideon responds.

"Cool. Now, does anyone know when our food is supposed to arrive?" Josué jokes and the tension dissipates.

I give him an appreciative smile. His speaking up gave me courage to do the same and defend the churches that raised us, albeit imperfectly. He smiles back, and it does something funny to my heart. I recognize this feeling.

I have a crush on him again.

Chapter 18

It's going well so far, I think. Pastor Aaron, my former youth pastor, has been offering insightful and encouraging questions regarding my ministry. He seems to understand the need and respect the work. Now, it's time to do the ask.

No matter how many times I do this part, and I've done it several times by now, it's always the most difficult aspect of a meeting.

"So, for me to do this full time, I depend on God to provide financial support as I'm not paid by Students for Jesus. I'm trusting God to raise up 57 people who support me financially at different levels on a monthly basis. God has already brought in 12 people. Would you be willing and able to be one of the remaining 45?"

He looks shocked. "Are you asking me for money?"

Oh gosh, this is uncomfortable. No one has reacted this way before. How do I even answer that? "In a way, yes. I'm asking if you'd be willing to support this ministry financially."

"How much money are you asking for?"

"Umm, any amount that you feel led to contribute-"

"No, in total." He cuts me off.

"Oh, about $3600 a month."

"That's a good amount of money, Gaelle. Do you even need all of that when you're still living at home?"

"Umm…" I don't even know what to say to that.

"You know, most pastors aren't even paid by the church. They work another job, sometimes another two, to provide for their families."

And those same pastors end up burnt out or neglecting their families. "Well-"

"You don't see them asking for money from hardworking people. No, they're willing to work extra hard instead."

He just interrupted me again. And is he trying to say that I'm not working hard? Raising financial support is hard work!

"I think that-" I try again.

"You know what, Gaelle. I'm not just surprised. I'm disappointed in you. How does your mother feel about you just going around begging people for money instead of working?"

I don't know if I'm more angry or sad at his words. "My manman is proud of me and the ministry that God has called me to. She supports me one hundred percent." He looks even more surprised than before. Time to end this time together. "I understand you don't agree with the ministry philosophy of raising financial support. Thank you for giving me your time to meet today." I try to end with a respectful tone, but my heart is equal parts seething and breaking.

"Well, you know I'm always one to speak my mind. Especially about matters as important as money. I hope that you'll reconsider your position because I think what you're doing is wrong." He gets up from the table.

"Okay, see you on Sunday."

"Yes, see you then." He says over his shoulder.

As soon as he leaves the Tim Hortons, I take a deep breath.

What just happened?

Did he really say that I'm begging? I asked politely. Did he really imply that I'm lazy and just not willing to work hard? Should I just look for another job to do when I'm not with students? But ministry already has such long hours. What time would I even have left over to work? When would I even sleep? But am I just being a leech or a burden to the people I've asked?

I'm so confused and feel so misunderstood.

Looking for a distraction, I take my phone out of my pocket and open my Instagram app. Maybe I can watch a funny reel or something. I see an unread message and go to it.

It's from Josué.

'Hey Gae. I just wanted to say thanks again for sending over the listening prayer stuff. I've been finding it helpful. I hope that you're doing well and can be encouraged that you are a blessing to people.'

This was a timely message. I'm not a leech. I'm a blessing to those around me. I type out a response.

'Hey Josué. Thanks for the message. I definitely needed it.'

There, done. As I gather my things to leave, I hear my phone chime. I pick it up to see that he's already

responded. I guess he's online.
'No problem. Did something happen, though? Are you okay?'

How honest do I want to be?
'I just had a really bad support appointment.'

His response is immediate.
'That sucks. Wanna meet up and process it?'

You know what? It's almost dinner, and it's not like I have a lot going on later. Why not?
'Sure, whereabouts?'

I'm in the York Region area for my support raising. Want to meet at the mall by our old high school?

That's actually near to the Tim Hortons that I'm at right now.
'Sounds good. I can be there in about 15 minutes.'

He replies almost instantly. *'Same. Meet you by the PB?'*

The Pickel Barrel? Where we had our first date?
'Sure, see you in 15!'

I smile at the phone as I close the app and put it back in my pocket. My mood has definitely lifted knowing that I can talk to someone about it who will get how crappy that was. I love Ruthia, but she just wouldn't understand this.

It's only when I'm pulling into a spot in the mall parking lot it hits me that this could fall under date territory. I shake my head to dislodge the thought. This is just two friends, two colleagues, meeting to discuss work. That's all.

When I walk through the mall entrance doors, I see him waiting for me by the hostess's podium. He gives me a big smile when he sees me, and I smile back. My heart flutters, and now it really feels like a date.

"Your table is ready," the hostess says to Josué and motions for us to follow her.

"I didn't realize we were eating here." I mention to him when we're seated.

"Oh shoot. Sorry for presuming." He looks chagrined. "I was just hungry and remembered that the food here is good."

"No worries. I don't mind, I like their food too." I still remember when we were first here. "It'll be a treat."

"Phew." He looks relieved. "Does that mean you already know what you want to order?"

"Yep, I love their fettuccine. What about you?"

"I'm going to go with steak tonight."

"Steak? That's fancy. I thought you were a missionary." I joke.

"Sorry, I ran out of Mr. Noodles and clean tap water." He says dryly, and I laugh.

"No clean drinking water, you've aced your missionary validity test." He joins me in laughter.

"Well, you two are a happy duo!" I look up to see a portly older woman in front of our table. "Hiya, my name is Gabby and I'm your server for tonight. Can I start with getting either of you something to drink?"

"Hi Gabby, I'll have a ginger ale, please. And I think we're good for ordering our meals now, too," Josué says warmly.

"Gotta love an efficient pair. Lay them on me." We give her our orders, and then she takes our menus. "I'll be back with your drinks and your food in a little while."

"Great, thank you Gabby!"

She smiles at us and then walks away.

"So, now that we've got that out of the way. What happened to your appointment?"

I sigh. I had almost forgotten the reason we were here. "He said that I was begging for money and that I should get a second job to supplement my income because that's what a hard worker would do."

"Yikes."

"Yep."

"How did you respond?"

"You mean when he wasn't interrupting me?"

"Double yikes."

"Yeah, I thanked him for his time and told him I would see him on Sunday at church."

"That's going to be fun." His sarcasm makes me chuckle.

"No kidding."

"You know it's not true, though, right? You're not a lazy beggar."

I swipe away at a few tears his words bring on. "Thanks. He got in my head, but then I was like, when would I sleep? You know what I mean? As ministers of the gospel, we work such long hours, and I'm supposed to add another job on top of that? It makes no sense."

"You're right. Many people want to cite Paul

working as a tentmaker for why people in ministry should work multiple jobs, but Paul only ever did that once, and that was temporarily. The rest of his ministry was just being an apostle full-time. He even says that the church should be supporting him and the others, but that he is choosing not to exercise that right. It's all in first Corinthians chapter 9."

"Okay, sir, you better preach!"

He laughs. "I get heated because I've heard it all before, as I have been raising support off and on for the last few years. It sucks that people don't get that we have a Biblical right to be supported that we're choosing to exercise so that we can live out the Biblical mandate given to us."

"Trust me, I don't mind it. It's nice to have someone get angry on my behalf with scripture to boot."

"Anytime. Was this your first time encountering pushback like this in your process?"

"Yeah, that's why it was so disorienting. Not everyone I've met with has come on financially, but they were all okay with the idea of me asking. Although, maybe they felt the way he did and just didn't want to say anything."

"Well, you'll never know what was in their hearts, and it does you no good to speculate about it. Just keep being faithful to meeting with people and ask. The worst is over. It can only go up from here."

At this moment, Gabby comes with our drinks, smiles, and then disappears.

"You know what? You're right. If this was my biggest fear, then it's already happened, and I've survived. The world didn't fall apart. I can keep going.

Thanks for that perspective." I take a big drink of my Coke.

"You're welcome, Gae. I'm just glad that I can help."

I can hear his care for me in his voice, and I feel my face warm. Here he is, just being a good friend to me and, my heart is going crazy with this crush.

I can't help it though. If I liked him before when we didn't even have this spiritual synchronicity, it's harder not to like him now.

It's time to change the subject, get him to stop staring at me with those eyes and that smile.

"What were your thoughts on our most recent staff training on the concepts model for sharing the gospel?"

"Oh." He seems startled by my question. I wonder where his mind was. "It was good. Sometimes we Gen Z-ers can give things like gospel sharing booklets a bad rap, but they were effective for the time that they were, and they're very clear about the different aspects of the gospel message."

"Yeah, I agree. I'm just not sure how crazy relevant they are to life now, though? Like, it's hard to just dive in and have a discussion with someone about the four spiritual laws right away."

"Oh, for sure. That's why I like to ask a general question about God or spirituality first and then dive into the booklet."

"You still use it?" I can't hide my surprise.

"Oh, yeah, sometimes at least. You don't, ever?"

"No, I feel like we have more effective tools than it, I guess."

"That's it. I'm daring you to use the booklet in the next week."

I laugh at this. "You dare me?"

"Yep. I even have one for you, so you can't claim that you don't have access to one." Before I can protest, he goes into his satchel and pulls out a *Knowing God Personally* booklet.

"Oh my gosh. Why do you have that on you?"

"You never know when an opportunity may present itself."

I shake my head. "You're wild."

"For the Lord." He says with a wink, and I can't help but laugh.

"The image that comes to mind is of John the Baptist. Should I ask Gabby to bring some locusts and honey instead of steak?" I tease.

He laughs at this. "Listen, his diet aside, mans was the greatest prophet to live! It's an honour to be thought of as someone like him, trust."

"Fair enough."

Then Gabby comes with our food. After placing them down in front of us, she steps back from the table at a respectful distance. "Do you guys need anything else?"

"No, thank you, Gabby." Josué says congenially, but I notice the glint in his eye.

When she walks away, I look at him. "What's going on in that mind of yours, Josué?"

"I think you should share the gospel with Gabby."

"Really?"

"Really. I just have a sense, is all. I would do it, but you have a dare to take care of."

"Okay, okay. When we get our bills, I'll see about initiating a spiritual conversation. Happy?"

"Ecstatic. Here, let me pray for our food."

After he prays, we dig in. It's delicious, per usual. We're silent as we eat, but comfortably so. I appreciate it as I seek the Lord for how to go about this upcoming spiritual conversation. I land on the question that I'll ask when Gabby shows up to check in on us.

"Are you guys good? Food is alright?"

"Yes, thank you, Gabby. We might even be ready for our bills." Josué raises an eyebrow at me to check-in, and I nod my head in agreement.

"Okay, I'll be back soon." She heads off to print them off.

"Alright, are you ready for this?" He looks so excited, and I can't lie; the nerves have given way to excitement in me, too.

"Yes. We'll see how it goes. Care to pray?"

"Of course. Holy Spirit, we pray You would be at work in Gabby's heart. Make her receptive to a spiritual conversation and give Gaelle an opportunity to share the gospel with her, in Jesus' name, amen."

Maybe five minutes later, Gabby returns with the machine. I gesture for Josué to take it first and while he does his stuff, I turn to her. "So Gabby, I know this is pretty random, but I had a question that I wanted to ask you. You don't have to answer it if you don't feel comfortable."

"Sure, go ahead. I'm a pretty open book."

"Well, if you could ask God any question, what would it be?"

"Oh wow, I was not expecting that, but it's a good question. Let me think about it for a moment."

Josué finishes paying and hands her back the terminal. She sets it up for me and sends it my way, silent the whole time. By the time I'm done paying, I'm wondering if she will answer the question at all. I'm about to say that she doesn't have to when she speaks.

"I think I would want to know how he feels about me. Like, does he care about me at all? Am I important or valuable to him? Something along those lines."

She says these words lightly, but I can hear the undercurrent of sadness. It pricks my heart. "Oh, Gabby. As a Christian, one of our core beliefs is that God has a deep love for every human. I believe that God more than just cares about you, He loves you."

At my words, she begins to tear up. "No one's ever told me that before."

"Would you be interested in hearing more about God's love and what that means for you, Gabby?" I ask her, offering her an unused napkin.

She nods. "I would."

"Well, I have a little booklet that breaks it down. Would it be okay if we read that together? Will you get in trouble for sitting beside me?"

"I shouldn't get in trouble. And if I do, I'm okay with that. This is important."

While she sits beside me, I pull out the booklet that Josué just gave me and read through it together as it details God's love, our sin, His response to our sin problem in Jesus' life, death and resurrection, and our response to believe in Him. When we get there, I check in with Gabby on where she's at.

"I think I want to believe in Jesus, but I still have questions. Is that okay?"

"That's completely okay. How about we exchange numbers, and we can meet up to explore some of those questions together?"

"That sounds great."

We do just that and then Josué and I get up to leave.

"Thank you again, Gabby, for your service toda,." Josué says.

"Are you kidding? Thank you for sharing about God's love with me! I'm excited to learn more."

We wave goodbye to her and then exit the restaurant. It's only when we're outside the mall that I shriek. "That was so cool! I need more of those booklets!"

Josué laughs. "It was cool to see the Holy Spirit use you. You're a natural evangelist."

"Thanks for pushing me. I'll keep you posted on her progress."

"Sweet. Well, I guess this is bye?"

Oh yeah, our non-date is now over. "I guess. See you in training?"

He nods and waves before walking away, taking a bit of my heart with him.

Chapter 19

You're here for Eleora. *You're here for Eleora. He might not even be at this service. Relax.* I repeat to myself as I exit my car and walk towards the entrance to Agape Community Church.

"Gaelle?" I turn to see Josué looking at me, surprised. "What are you doing at Agape?"

The familiar pitter patter of my heart ensues, and I hold in a dreamy sigh. He dresses up for church! As if he wasn't attractive enough in shorts and a t-shirt.

"Eleora's performing a poem today, and I thought I'd come to support her. Plus, I've never been here before. I want to understand what all the hype is about."

"Oh, cool! Chad didn't mention that, but maybe it was supposed to be hush hush."

"Oops. Now that I've told you, I guess I have to kill you."

"Well, to die is gain, right? I guess I should say thank you?"

We laugh together as we enter the church building. "Here, the sanctuary is on the right."

"Where do you sit?" I ask him as I follow him into a large room filled with chairs.

"With Chad and the other young adults. So, you'll be able to see Eleora, Amy and Cass."

"Perfect. Lead the way!"

We walk towards the right side of the sanctuary a few rows from the front, and I see my girls. I give a wave, and Amy sees me first.

"Ahh! You're here!" She shrieks, nudging Cass beside her.

"Who's here?" Amy points me out, walking towards them, and Cass gives me a big smile.

"Gaelle! Welcome!" I go to the row behind them since theirs is full and we exchange hugs. "Are you here for Ellie?"

"I am. She sounded super nervous in the group chat, so I figured I'd come and show support."

"That's wonderful. She just went to the bathroom for, like, the fifth time, but I'm sure she'll be glad to see you when she comes back."

"Sweet." I sit down, and surprisingly, Josué sits beside me.

"You're not going to sit with your guys?" I gesture to Gideon and Chadwick.

"Nah, their row is pretty full. Unless you don't want me to sit beside you because my deodorant isn't working or something."

"That's the reason. Don't tell me you're one of those people that don't believe in real deodorant, are you?" I lob back and we laugh.

Then I notice Eleora coming up the aisle, her face paler than normal. "Ellie!"

She moves her head to the sound of my voice and then breaks into a big smile. "You came for me?"

I give her a big hug once she reaches me. "I did.

You're going to kill it. I know that for sure. But even if you don't, you'll still be so loved."

"Thank you. I needed to hear that."

"No problem." We smile at each other and then she moves into the row ahead of me to sit beside Chadwick. As soon as she gets to him, he reaches for her hand and gives it a comforting squeeze. She smiles up at him, and he gives a quick kiss on the forehead.

They are too cute.

I sit back down and turn my attention away from them before envy can taint the beautiful scene I'd just witnessed.

Just in time, too, since the countdown on the screen reaches zero, and the band is ready for us.

The musical worship is actually fantastic. It's very Christian contemporary, but the musicality is excellent, and the songs are rich with wonderful truth. As it winds down, I notice Eleora get up from her seat and make her way to the front.

She looks in our direction and I shoot her a double thumbs up. She smiles, takes a deep breath and then speaks.

"I refuse to be gnostic. I know this is an archaic word.

It doesn't reside in our daily vocabularies, not like lit, triggered, woke, or thirsty

but it shows up in our modern worldview.

It means to deny the good of the material world, of the body.

I refuse to let my body be

Devalued. Diminished. Dismissed.

I call my body good. I call my body holy.
So, worship happens in sanctuaries and hair salons.
Zumba classes and cathedrals.

I refuse to let sex be reduced to a carnal, physical act.
Covenantal, complementary, charitable love makes the Creator smile.
Anything else is blasphemy.

This means that I could never be content with sameness
or self or screen

Somehow, we are all gnostic.
We choose digital worlds instead of being present.
We hustle to complete our to do lists and run our bodies ragged.

We don't sleep enough.
Take vitamins. Floss.
We live like our bodies don't matter.

We ignore neurochemical imbalance and label it lack of faith.
We take Advil for migraines and get massages for soreness.
But neglect to care for existential questions that are fuelling those aches.

We treat bodies like they're just biology. And not

theology.

We forget the image of God imprinted upon us from within the womb.

We make humanity into cells.

We create prison cells for ourselves and call it our truths.

Gnostics can never be lit. Or triggered,
because they have no grounding in the real world.

No real pleasure, no real pain.
Gnosticism is colour blind.
What is culture and ethnicity and diversity if we are all disembodied consciousnesses?

Gnostics can't wake because they don't rest.
Gnostics don't thirst.
Don't have needs to be satisfied.

They do,
but they've sought satisfaction in denying the needs
instead of getting them met.

Gnosticism is an archaic word
but a modern reality.
I choose an "archaic" reality instead.

I choose wonder. I choose to be embodied.
I choose the paradox that to be human is physical and spiritual
and not just one or the other.

I refuse to be gnostic.
I choose to be human.
I choose to be Christian."

You could hear a pin drop in the room and then we burst into applause. "Whoo!" I cheer as she gives us all a big smile before putting the mic back and walking to her seat.

I knew she liked to write, but I didn't realize that she was that talented. My Lord, what a gift! I'm going to ask her for a copy of the poem later as there was so much to chew on from it.

As the applause dies down, a South Asian man comes onto the stage. "Praise God for the gift of poetry, amen?"

"Amen!" I call out with a few other people.

"Well, I'm Tav for those who don't know me, and today we're starting our series on First John. We'll be in the first four verses today. If you can, please stand for the reading of God's Word."

I swipe to First John on my phone and then stand.

After reading the passage, to my surprise, Tav kneels down on the stage. "Triune God, we thank You for Your Word. Help us, I pray, to glean from it what You would have for us. May I be an effective communicator and not a barrier to anyone who hears my voice? May Your Word find our hearts to be good soil. Glorify Yourself in this time of preaching. Amen." Amens echo across the room. "You guys may be seated. There are two main points that I'm going to get into today. The first is titled Testify, and the second is Joyful Fellowship."

From that point on, I'm hooked. He breaks down

why it was so significant that the disciples tangibly witnessed Jesus pre-crucifixion and post-resurrection: the philosophical perspective of Gnosticism. Tension he explains what that means and how we see it today, which is so convicting! He closes with discussing salvation and evangelism, and then prays for us.

Once Tav finishes doing so, the worship team comes back on and does a few more songs and then we're dismissed. "Okay, I get the hype. This was a great service!" I say to Josué with a huge smile on my face.

He smiles back. "I'm glad that you enjoyed it, Gae." Even though he's said the right words, something about him seems off, but I can't put my finger on it.

"I really did. Ooh! I've got to tell Eleora that she did a great job. Be right back."

"No worries."

I rush to Eleora and give her a big hug. "I knew you would kill it! You slayed that!"

"Thank you. Thank you." She looks embarrassed but also proud of herself. "Do you think you'll want to join us for brunch after church? There's an IHOP not too far from here."

"Bet. I'll be there."

"Did you like the service other than my poem?"

"Oh yeah! It was great. If I lived in Brampton, I'd go here too. It doesn't hurt that so many people I love already go here."

"True. Well -" Eleora is interrupted as an older man who shares her eyes lifts her up from behind.

"What the -?" She squiggles to turn around and then laughs. "Dad! What the heck? I didn't know it was you."

"I'm so proud of you, baby girl. I had to tell you ASAP." That is adorable. I decide to take my leave, knowing that I'll see her at the IHOP later. I return to Josué, who has a contemplative look on his face.

"So, that sermon though. Is Tav always so on point when he preaches?"

Josué nods. "Yeah, I feel like with him I truly see that teaching is a spiritual gift! What stood out to you from the sermon?"

I look over my notes. "My fingers were flying to capture one of his explanations word for word. Here it is, 'Anytime that we ignore, downplay, or harm our bodies, we are engaging in a form of Gnosticism. Being embodied matters, for Jesus and for us.' The way he tied it to sexual immorality, exercise and nutrition, ethnicity and biological sex – and even mental health! I loved all the application points that he drew out."

"Agreed. That was fire!"

I smile at his enthusiasm. It's great to have someone to process a sermon with. "What about you? What's sticking with you from the message?"

"Oh!" He seems flustered. "I liked the way he highlighted evangelism as an application point. There is so much joy in sharing the joy of our salvation and I think a lot of people don't realise that."

"You're absolute right. That practical suggestion to think of five non-Christians in our lives and consistently pray for them was wonderful! This church is huge! If even a quarter did this suggestion, that would be like 1000 unbelievers being prayed for. That's amazing!" I'm expecting him to match my enthusiasm, so when he's silent, I grow concerned. "Hey, are you okay?"

"Yeah, I'm just … well… First off, I could barely focus on the sermon today."

I feel my brows furrow. "Oh?"

"It was hard to focus with you sitting beside me, looking so stunning, smelling so good, and taking such copious notes. That last one might have been the most attractive of the three."

"Attractive?" What is he saying? I have to sit down.

He joins me and continues speaking, "Yes. Your passion for ministry, your gentle boldness in evangelism, your sound theology, your enthusiasm for the Kingdom. Everything about you that I was attracted to before is still there, but now there's only more of you that I'm drawn to. It's driving me crazy." He sighs and takes a deep breath. "I would like to ask you to go on a date with me."

This is what being in shock feels like. "You what?"

"I really like you, Gaelle. And I would like us to explore being more than colleagues and family in the faith. How do you feel about that? Do you think you could give me a chance again?"

Is this happening? The guy I like likes me back? Again? I feel like I'm dreaming.

"Are you kidding?" His face falls, and I realize how that probably sounded like a rejection. "No. I mean yes! Yes, I'll go out with you."

I see his expression change from sad to cautiously hopeful. "You will?"

"I will." I say firmly.

"Yes!" He exclaims and pumps his fist, making some people around us stare at him quizzically.

"You're being a goofball," I tease.

"And you like it." He volleys back.

I feel myself beginning to blush. "Yeah, I guess I do." He pumps his fist again, and I laugh.

I'm so glad that I visited Agape today.

Chapter 20

'*You look beautiful* today, per usual.' I smile at the message from Josué that came in just as I signed onto our new staff training call. Before I reply, another message comes in: '*I love I can make you smile like that. I'm fist pumping right now on the inside.*'

I look up at the screen and he gives me a wink, making me laugh. If this is how giddy he already makes me, how much more will it be on or after our "first" date?

"Alright, it looks like everyone is here. Annie, can you start us off by praying for us today?" Victoria opens up our time.

"Sure. Heavenly Father, we thank you for the opportunity to be in vocational ministry amongst students. Be with Victoria as she leads this time and would we receive all that You have for us today. Amen."

"Amen. Thank you, Annie. Today, we're going to talk about the Engagement Model which you would've watched a short video on to prepare for this time. Intervarsity Staff developed it, also known as the Five Thresholds. It's important to remember as we dive into this that the Engagement model is neither a science nor a law, just an observed pattern amongst those who have come to faith in Jesus in recent years. It can help us understand where non-Christians are at in their spiritual journey, which helps us to know how to journey with them well." She pauses and I nod along with my peers. I'm familiar with the Engagement Model, but it never hurts to have a refresher.

And with that, we're off. It's great to learn from my peers and become aware of some of my evangelism blindspots.

Shortly after the call, I get another message from Josué.

That was so good that I had to abandon my plan to message you throughout the training.

I have to laugh at this.
LOL. I see how it is. Sharing the gospel is more important than flirting with me?

His message comes back immediately.
You know you wouldn't have it any other way, lool. ;)

He's right. I wouldn't.
Stop being right, it's annoying.

His response comes after a few minutes, which feels like ages compared to only a few seconds.

I've gotten a lot of things wrong. I'm trying to get it all right this time around. You're worth it.

Well, how is a girl supposed to argue with that? Before I can respond, another message comes in.

How would you feel about a phone call? We didn't have a breakout time for this training and I'm dying to debrief / process it with someone. Sunday showed me that you're a great debriefing partner!

My heart hammers in my chest at the idea of talking to him on the phone. I need to calm down. We're talking about our shared work. I don't need to make it a bigger deal than it is.

Sure, I'm down for a call. Do you need my number? It's the same from high school.

Immediately, my phone rings with an unknown but slightly familiar number.

"Hi?" my voice is tentative.

"Do I seem like a stalker for still having your number?"

I laugh at Josué's first words. "You definitely don't."

"Phew. Okay, what stood out to you from the training?"

"Too many things to mention, we might have to go by each threshold."

"I like that idea, Gae. Okay, for the first one, building trust, I like how you mentioned leading out in vulnerability as a way to foster trust."

I'm flattered that he remembered me saying that.

"Thanks! I appreciated the reminder that what's important at that stage is to be a good friend. For the sparking curiosity threshold, I remember you bringing up living counter-culturally as a way to build curiousity. I loved that. Our witness has to include words, but it needs actions too!"

"Yes! It's definitely a both-and, not an either-or."

I'm nodding emphatically and then I remember that he can't see me right now. "I am nodding in agreement."

He laughs and I feel its vibrations down to my toes. "Good to know. I also appreciated how Victoria clarified for us the difference between curiousity and seeking. It's really easy for me to confuse the two."

"I feel you on that. I took notes on what she said. 'Curiosity is asking questions about spiritual things or faith. Seeking is normally accompanied by an intentional understanding of Jesus.' I needed that reminder too. As a missionary, it's so easy to want to jump the gun!"

"You're right. It's a balance between having urgency and rushing someone's faith journey. How was threshold three for you?"

I think about his question. "It's tricky! I find it hard to challenge people to help them realise their lives need to change. The directness that it requires is jarring and uncomfortable for me."

"You are a pretty gentle person, Gaelle, which is a strength – not a weakness. There are way too many aggressive missionaries."

I feel so seen right now. Not exposed or ashamed, but known and embraced. "Thank you."

"You're welcome. Now, thresholds four and five are probs the ones we love the most, but the ones I've seen the least. Someone actually seeking and then making a decision to follow Jesus is wild to me!"

"I know! Most people I know are still learning to

trust Christians or be curious about spiritual things. It would be such a privilege to accompany someone in their seeking or pray with someone to come to faith."

"God willing, we'll both get to experience that someday."

"Yeah. I'm believing for that, anyway." We sit in silence for a moment. I wonder what he's thinking about.

"I'm really glad that we had this call, Gaelle. I've always loved your voice but now it's like it speaks to my spirit too, not just my soul. Does that make sense?"

His words are like sunshine and water. My heart feels like it's blooming in my chest. "It does. It's a gift that we share such similar callings and assignments. It makes empathy easy."

"I love how you worded that, Gae." He pauses. "I should probably let you go – even though I don't want to. I look forward to our date in a few days, though. Until then, my empathy buddy."

I laugh at the adorable endearment. "See you soon, Josué."

"I still love the way you say my name." His voice is husky. There's a tension in my body that wasn't there before. A longing for intimacy that hasn't been present for years. "Goodbye for now."

He hangs up before I can respond. I stare at the phone in surprise at what's happening within me through a simple phone call.

What will happen on our actual date?

Chapter 21

The first thing I notice when I pick Josué up is how bright his shoes are. They're white Adidas sneakers and they look like they've never been worn. Was he saving them for a special occasion?

Is being on a date with me a special occasion to him?

I'm so lost in my thoughts that I don't realize that he's been speaking to me.

"Gaelle? You okay?"

No one should look so handsome when they're concerncd about you.

"Yeah, just, umm, nice shoes?"

"Thanks." The smile that lights his face confirms for me they probably are new, and he's happy that I noticed.

"So, where to?"

"Well, I have a picnic packed for us, but I don't have drinks. We can go to a Starbucks that's on the way to a park, I know, if that works out for you." It's only then do I realize he has a backpack with him. My heart flutters at his thoughtfulness.

"Sounds like a plan. Should I bring out google maps or will you be our navigator?"

"How about both? I'll manage google maps and direct you."

"Presumptuous of you in assuming that we have that kind of trust already developed." I make my voice teasing so that he knows that I'm not serious, and he laughs.

"At least I'm not asking you to wear a blindfold."

"Solid Licence to Wed reference, Josué." I raise my eyebrow at him in surprise.

"Thank you. Being solo parented by your mom will give one a rich knowledge of classic rom coms."

"Yep, that'll do it. How is your mom, by the way? Also, which direction should I be heading in?"

"Oh, you want to get on the highway, heading south on the 410 and then west on the 401."

"Gotcha. That's all I need to know. I'll check back in for more directions when the time comes." I put the car in drive and begin heading towards the highway.

"As for my mom, she's okay. She's recovered now from my decision to go into vocational ministry."

"Recovered?"

"Oh, she wasn't happy about it. I ruined her Immigrant Dream for me to have a successful, well-paying job upon graduation."

"I'm sorry." I had my manman's support from the get-go. I couldn't imagine having to navigate her disapproval of my ministry calling.

"Don't be. It was God's sanctification plan for us both. I needed to obey Him more than my mom, and she needed to surrender my future into God's hands. It's been good for us to disagree and wrestle with each other on this."

"I like how you put that. 'God's sanctification

plan'. Isn't it amazing that He's gracious enough towards us to reveal parts of his sanctification plan to us? Like, He doesn't have to give us the reason He's allowing something to happen, but He does anyway."

He's so quiet after I share that I give him a quick glance to make sure that he's okay and see him just smiling warmly at me. "I appreciate that I can talk with you about God-related things, and it's not 'too much' for you."

"If anything, it's not enough. Tell me what you've been learning in your quiet times with Jesus."

We talk about our respective gleanings from our times with God for the rest of the drive. After going through a Starbucks drive through, Josué checks in with me. "How hungry are you right now?"

"Hmmm. Not much, to be honest."

"Feel like taking a pit stop at RONA?"

It's so random that I laugh. "What's at RONA?"

"What isn't at RONA?" He counters.

"Ummm. A lot of things. I can list them if you'd like."

"Just trust me and pull in here." He says, gesturing to the RONA entrance on my right.

My shoulders shaking from laughter, I do as he said and find a parking spot near the entrance and cut the engine. "Okay, now what?"

"Now, we go gardening!" He says and exits the car.

He comes around to my side and opens the door for me, extending a hand towards me to help me out. Smiling at the gesture, I take his hand and am surprised at a slight tug that lands me flush against him, right into his arms. They encircle me, his hands on my lower back. I bring my hands to his shoulders. It's easy to relax into his touch.

Somehow, it's both familiar and exhilarating being this close to him.

I look up to see a sheepish look on his face. "Is this okay? I was so eager to hold you, I didn't even check first," he admits.

"It actually isn't okay." His face falls, and he moves his arms away. "It's much, much better than that." I add and then lean my head against his shoulder.

His hold on me tightens, and I feel his head come to rest on my shoulder. We're not doing anything indecent, and yet the moment feels radically intimate. The butterflies in my stomach are at rest, like the whole of me knows that I'm safe with him.

I'm not sure how long we stand like that in the RONA parking lot. It's only when we hear a car honk that we break apart.

It's a warm June day, and yet I shiver without his warmth.

"I didn't know a hug could feel like that. Oh crap. I just said that out loud, didn't I?"

I can't help but laugh at this, and the weight of the moment we just shared becomes lighter. "That no–filter thing hasn't changed in the last few years, eh?" I tease him.

He chuckles. "I guess not. Are you ready for some gardening?"

"Sure." I walk towards the entrance to the store, but Josué shakes his head.

"Nope, we're not going inside. We're going to the garden centre on the other side of the parking lot."

"And you let me park here, knowing this?"

"I needed to increase my daily step count," he says dryly, and I laugh.

"Okay, lead the way."

I follow him to a corner of the parking lot that's been dedicated to flowers upon flowers upon flowers. "Whoa."

"Yep, it's a gardener's dream."

"Since when do you garden?" I ask him.

"I'm a Caribbean male. How could I not garden?"

"Is that a thing?"

"I think so. At least in my family, my dad used to have a vegetable garden, and both my granddads have those as well."

"Learn something new every day."

"That's the right attitude. So, are you ready to design our fictitious garden?"

"Let's do this!" What I lack in knowledge, I make up for in enthusiasm.

We spend the next half an hour looking at all the flowers. I'm drawn to whatever looks pretty and then he explains what kind of flower it is. It's a blast. We even spot a Black garden gnome that we both agree needs to be in our garden, guarding the precious flowers. At the end of our perusing, he ends up buying the gnome. Once he finishes paying, he gives it to me. "For you and our future garden."

My heart speeds up at the word 'future' and all its implications as I take the gnome into my arms.

"Thank you. Shall we head over to your picnic spot now?"

"You're welcome. And sure! It's only a few minutes away from here." We head back to the car and, true to his word, we are at a beautiful park that's right beside a picturesque, small lake.

"This is gorgeous." I comment.

"Like recognizes like."

My cheeks warm as he looks shocked. "What the heck? Why do I keep doing that?"

"I don't mind the cheese. It's not like I'm lactose intolerant." I joke, and he smiles.

"That's good to know. Do you want to pick our spot?"

I nod my head and find a spot under a tree that's right by the water.

"Nice choice."

"I've been training all my life for this moment, so I'm glad it's paid off." I deadpan and he laughs, taking a blanket out of the backpack and spreading it out on the grass.

I sit on the blanket as he takes out food. We have croissant sandwiches, fruit and chocolate.

"Not as epic as our first picnic, I know." He says almost apologetically.

Time to nip that in the bud.

"Are you kidding? This looks great. Thank you for preparing it for us."

"You're welcome. Shall we pray and dig in?"

"Sure. Go ahead." I say, bowing my head and closing my eyes.

I am pleasantly surprised when I feel him take one of my hands. "Father, thank You for this food and for this opportunity to spend time together. Bless both in Jesus' name, amen."

"Amen," I whisper and look up to see a content smile on his face.

"Alright, time to see if these are any good." He

jokes and hands me a croissant sandwich on a napkin. "There's turkey, lettuce and cheese. I made yours without mayo."

I'm touched that he remembered I don't like mayo. "Sounds perfect."

We eat in silence for the next few minutes, giving me a chance to check out our surroundings a bit more. While it's a beautiful spot, it pales compared to the image-bearer lying down in front of me. It's my first time seeing him in a sleeveless shirt and I notice he has a few tattoos that he definitely didn't have 6 years ago.

"Can you tell me about your tattoos?" I ask him after I polish off my sandwich.

"Sure." He points to the one on his shoulder. "This is a symbol from Ghana called gye nyame. It means God is present or with us. I chose a Ghanaian symbol because most Jamaicans were brought over from Ghana via the transatlantic chattel slave trade. I wanted something on my body that reflected God and was a part of my identity. Not that slavery is my identity, but it's a part of my ancestral history, and I wanted to honour my ancestors in this way."

"I think that's beautiful, Josué. What about this one?" I point to a tattoo that is the length of his forearm. It looks like a detailed wavy sword.

"This one is based on Damascus steel. It's made through the process of hammering, folding, throwing back into the furnace, taking it out, then hammering and folding it again, over and over until it's finished. Through that process, it creates this beautiful pattern, and it's one of the strongest steels in the world. I chose this one because, for me, that's what the process of sanctification is like. It can be brutal, hard and painful at times, like this steel being thrown into the fire, hammered, folded and repeat. But in the end, it's beautiful, and we become a powerful tool in the hands of the Father for His purposes and glory."

"I love that so much! Normally, I hear the process of refining described with gold. You know, God heats us up in the fire and then removes the dross from the top to make us more pure. This, though, feels like it takes the work of God to another level. A more honest level."

It's hard to place how he's looking at me. It's part awe, part respect, and part understanding? "Exactly! Like, sometimes life is more painful than that metaphor implies."

We share a look of understanding, and I feel like, once again, we've stumbled upon an intimate moment. The tension is so tangible that it feels like I could feel it if I stretched out my hand between us. He's the first to look away and clear his throat.

"So, yeah, those are my tattoos. I've been wondering, how has support raising been going for you - aside from that one crappy appointment?"

A total gear shift, but I'm alright with it. "I'm just over halfway at 57%." I tell him and reach for some fruit.

"That's amazing, Gae! You're on track to be done by late August." He does his adorable fist pump, and I can't help but laugh at how genuinely excited he is for me. "How are you feeling about the entire process?" he asks.

"Hmmm. It's so difficult asking for money and following up and being ghosted. But also, it's incredible to share the vision of this ministry with people and see them get excited about reaching international students. Sometimes, I think I'm even going to miss doing support raising. Does that sound crazy?"

"Not at all. My support raising coach last year taught me that this is our ministry to the church, and that always stuck with me."

"I've heard that too. I'm speaking at my church this Sunday about my ministry, so that's, like, a very obvious way that this process ministers to the church."

"That's great, Gae. I hope that it's a fruitful opportunity. Churches can be tricky. It can be slow for them to join your giving team, but once they do, they're with you for a while and the amount is larger than individual people. Do you already have what you're going to say ready?"

"Sort of? I have some work to do on it over the next few days." I shrug.

"You don't sound nervous about this at all. Have you done a lot of public speaking?"

"A few times in my undergrad I spoke at a worship night or at our weekly meetings on campus."

"Ahh, so you're a veteran. You have a process that you know works for you for this kind of stuff."

This comment makes me snort, which makes him laugh. "I'm definitely not a veteran, but I'm okay speaking in front of people."

He nods his head in understanding. "And here I was about to ask about coming to offer you moral support, which it doesn't seem you need."

I laugh at this. "Is this you fishing for an invitation, Josué?"

"Maybe."

"Well, you are welcome to come to my church and

see me present this Sunday if you're free."

"I'll have to check my calendar." He makes a big show of checking his phone, causing me to laugh even more. "Okay, I'll be there." He says with a cheeky grin.

I smile back at him. "Great."

"Okay, honesty time."

"Alright, I guess I'll have to stop lying to you, then." I say dryly, and he laughs.

"What were your first thoughts when you saw me at NST?"

I wasn't expecting this question. I try my best to go back to that moment. "Well, I was in shock."

"Right, that makes sense."

"And," my face warms as I remember what I was thinking.

"And?"

How do I word this without sounding like I was objectifying him or something? "That you looked good." I decide to say.

He laughs heartily at this.

"Okay, what about you? What did you think when you saw me again?" I ask him.

"That God might be even kinder than I imagined to potentially be giving me another chance with you and then a prayer that I wouldn't blow it. How am I doing so far?"

He's looking at me, so earnestly.

"So far, that prayer has been answered."

Josué smiles at me, and I feel transported into a cocoon of contentment, like nothing can go wrong right now. He's right, God is so so kind.

Chapter 22

Manman and I arrive at legliz for École du dimanche [*Sunday school*] that happens before the service begins. While the preaching isn't always verse by verse, Sunday school is 45 minutes where we get into the meat of the text, so we always try to leave early enough to attend.

"Koman fanmi an yé [*how's the family*]?" A woman around my mom's age says to us.

"Fanmi-an byen [*the family is doing well*]." My mom responds and the two speak in rapid Kreyol.

"Koman ou yé, Gaelle [*how are you*]?" A voice says behind me.

I turn around to see Emmanuel, a guy a little older than me, with his grandmother on his arm. Manman likes to tease me about him sometimes, saying that he likes me. He's nice enough, but my heart has never reacted to him in any way other than friendship. Although the way he dotes on his grandmother is endearing.

"Ko-a pa pi mal [*we are doing alright*]." I respond and then turn to his grandmother. "Koman ou santi ko-a [*how are you feeling today*]?"

She gives me a warm smile at the customary

greeting for the elderly. "Mwen byen [*I am okay]*.

"I'm glad to hear that. I'll see you inside?" The nerves over my upcoming presentation are making me antsy. I very much feel the need for École du dimanche to help instil some peace from God's Word.

They nod at me, and I decide to shortcut any other greetings and head inside the sanctuary. I go to our normal spot by the band and then take some deep breaths. I am okay. I will do just fine. God is with me. I have nothing to worry about.

Manman comes to sit beside me. She must realize that I'm freaking out because she takes one of my hands in her and gives me a reassuring squeeze. "I believe that you will do wonderfully, my not so little Gae Gae."

"Merci, Manman." I say, leaning my head onto her shoulder. While I eagerly pray for Don to become a Christian, I am at the same time happy that our faith is something that we can share, just the two of us.

Then, École du dimanche starts. Our pastor is going through Philippians 4 verses fifteen through nineteen, and he uses it to talk about giving. Ahh, maybe that's why he asked me to speak today. He wanted the church to have a direct way to apply the passage. When it ends, I'm feeling a bit more confident. The church has just heard about Biblical giving to people in ministry. It's a perfect layup for me.

I scan the room to see if Josué had arrived during the teaching, but I don't see him. I tried to tamp down my disappointment. He said he would come. I have to trust that he'll do what he said.

I notice Pastè [*pastor*] beckoning me to the sound booth and head over there. I'm given a mic and told how to turn it on for when it's time for me to speak. By the time we're done speaking, the worship team is on the stage, and I rush back to my seat. As we are invited to stand, I do one last scan of the room and see Josué moving to a row in the back. I want to wave, but don't want to draw attention to the fact that I'm not paying attention to what's happening right now.

I'm just so glad that he came.

The remaining nerves I have dissipate. This is how Eleora must've felt when she saw all of us there for her. Maybe I should've mentioned this talk in the chat so that they could support me. It feels weird though, I guess, to talk about support raising with them.

But it's easy with Josué and it's great to know that I have his and my manman's support. Like, God is giving me a tangible reminder of His support. For the next better part of an hour, the worship team leads us in songs of praise to our God. They're mostly old school Caribbean songs, but they throw in a couple of new ones too. Every few songs, someone comes up to read a portion of scripture. I'm especially blessed by the reading of Psalm 46:1-3 about God being near, so we don't need to be afraid.

I sure hope that Josué is enjoying himself. Having him be at my church feels like a new level of intimacy, like I'm letting him see another part of me.

It's scary and exhilarating all at once.

It's now time for the prière pastoral [*pastoral prayer*] where Pastè does a general intercessory prayer for the congregation. Through it I learn of cancer diagnoses, one person losing their foot to diabetes, and a new baby being born. He wraps up by praying for Canada and Justin Trudeau. It never ceases to amaze me that the congregation can sit through and focus upon a 15-minute prayer every week.

For tithes and offering time, the worship team comes back up and invites people to dance to the front to give their offering in the baskets in front of the stage. It's one of my favourite parts of the service; seeing such wholesome and joyful dancing makes my heart glad. During that time, I see Josué two stepping to the front. He flashes me a quick smile when he catches me looking, and I give him one right back.

Next, it's time for announcements. We are reminded of Wednesday night Bible Study, Friday night youth group, and jeune [*Saturday morning prayer*].

Then, I'm up. I walk up to the stage and flip on the mic I was given. For a moment, I'm frozen. Then I look to the back and see Josué doing a barely noticeable fist pump. Suddenly, I want to laugh, and I'm no longer frozen. I put my phone on the podium and open up the notes for my talk.

"Bonjou legliz! Mwen rele Gaelle [Good morning *church! My name is Gaelle]*, for those who don't know me. Today, I'll be speaking on missions at home. Mèsi to Pastè for the opportunity." And with that, I'm in the zone. Soon enough, I'm giving my closing remarks. "We have been more blessed than we could even imagine. We were born into a time and place where we were able to encounter the gospel and come into a relationship with God through the saving work of Jesus Christ. But we also have the privilege of participating in His plan for redeeming our brothers and sisters. So, let's do it! Mèsi everyone for your time!"

My mom is the first to clap and then stands up. Many others follow suit until it's the entire room. I turn off the mic and return to my seat, surrounded by smiles.

When I get to my seat, I check my phone again and see a message from Josué. *'You slayed that! I took a video for you if you want to share it with others.'*

It takes all my willpower not to turn around to see him and express my gratitude in that moment.

"Hey, hey, do I even need to preach when Gaelle just brought a word? We have a future pastè amongst us!" Pastè says jovially, and we all laugh. "What a reminder to empower the youth! They are our future!"

"Amèn!" someone calls out and manman gives me a quick shoulder squeeze.

"Okay, today we're going to be looking at..."

It's hard for me to focus upon the sermon, try as I might. When he finishes, I'm itching to get up and see Josué, but before I can, other people come to talk to me.

Some want to volunteer with the French language class I'm running, others want to host students, and a few are curious about supporting the ministry financially! I take down everyone's details and thank them again for their interest.

When they're all gone, I look to the back for Josué and don't see him. Did he leave without even saying hi? Disappointment rises in me until I feel a tap on my shoulder. I turn around to see him.

"You were Ms. Popular, so I figured I'd get in line." He teases. "But seriously, you did a great job and I'm glad people came to talk to you afterwards. That's awesome! I would give you a hug, but I think, given our environment, a high five may be more appropriate."

He holds up his hand, and I hit it lightly. I'd much rather be holding his hand, but he's right that this is not the place.

I'm about to ask him what he thought of the

service when I hear my manman say in an icy voice. "What is he doing here?"

Chapter 23

"Bonswa Mme Frances. How did you enjoy the service?"

Manman doesn't even look at him but turns her attention to me. "Well, Gaelle, I'm waiting."

"I told him I was speaking today, and he came to offer me support." I rush to explain.

"Since when are you two in contact with each other?"

I notice people are beginning to stare at the three of us. "Manman, can we not do this here?"

"It might be best if I get going. Bye Gaelle." He's putting up a good front, but I can tell that he's hurt.

"Talk to you later, Josué." I say with a wave, and he waves back.

"Yeah, later."

I turn to look at Manman and she is unimpressed by the exchange.

"Manman, I-"

"Let's get to the car, Gaelle."

She brokers no room for argument, heading towards the exit. I follow her silently.

When we get to the car, I aim to make another attempt to talk to her, but the look on her face makes me think twice. She's seething.

In some ways, her reaction to Josué feels like a blindside. On the other hand, maybe this is why I refrained from mentioning reconnecting with him. On some level, maybe I knew it would go badly, and I didn't see the point in bringing him up and all the emotional baggage that accompanies our past.

And then I started to like him again.

Maybe I should've told my manman then about him being back in my life. But I didn't expect him to like me back. Who expects for lightning to strike in the same place twice?

And that's what being with him feels like, electrifying and, at the same time, incredibly safe.

I sigh as it hits me that although I have all these reasons, or better yet excuses, for why I didn't tell her, they don't matter now. Now, what matters is cleaning up this mess that my passivity has made.

She's mad at me, and I hate this feeling of us not being okay. And I do not know how Josué's feeling, if he's angry with me too for not saying anything. Or, if he thinks it means that I don't care.

That would be so much worse than his anger.

Once we pull into the driveway, I build up the courage to start a conversation when we get inside the house. As soon as our shoes are off, I try again.

"Manman, can we talk now, please?"

She motions for us to go to the living room. When we arrive there, she sits on the loveseat, and I take the armchair. "Well, talk."

"Okay, so. First, he didn't post the pictures. Another classmate of his got access to his computer and posted them. He showed me the proof of that when we first reconnected."

"And when was this?"

"At New Staff Training. He's also a new staff member with Students for Jesus." I ready myself for her being upset at me withholding this information for so long.

"I thought you were working for a Christian organization."

Well, I didn't expect that. I'm a bit offended on SFJ's behalf. "I am. Josué is a Christian now. He has a cool testimony, actually."

"And you believe him? You believe he could be saved after what he did?"

I try to tamp down the anger I'm feeling. "Of course I do. The gospel is for sinners. No one comes to Jesus without ways they've sinned before, and He welcomes all to believe in Him. That's one of the most beautiful aspects of our faith!" I expect the beauty of the gospel to penetrate her cold exterior, but it does no such thing.

"What if he's manipulating you again?"

Now, I'm confused. "Again?"

"Well, how else did he get you to take those photos?"

Oh. *That.* "I volunteered, Manman." I cringe at this. Definitely wasn't a wise choice. "I loved him and decided. He didn't manipulate me into anything."

"Hmph." I'm not even sure what that's supposed to mean. I'm just about ready to end this conversation and check in on Josué, but then I realize there's more to disclose.

Sigh.

"I should also mention that he was the one I went

on that date with earlier this week."

She gasps, and her eyes widen in shock. "I thought you were with Emmanuel."

"Emmanuel? He's a nice guy, but I don't see him that way."

"Maybe that's because Satan is trying to distract you from who you're supposed to be with."

At this, I can't help but roll my eyes. "That's a jump, Manman. I like Josué. He's matured into quite a man of faith, and I enjoy being around him."

"No, absolutely not. You are not thinking clearly. You need to stop seeing him."

I'm the one that's not thinking clearly?

"Manman. You're being unreasonable."

"The Bible says to honour your father and mother. You need to obey me and not see him anymore."

"The Bible also says not to exasperate your children, Manman." I point out.

"I am protecting you, even though you don't see that yet. You don't have my permission or blessing to date Josué, so nip things in the bud as soon as possible." Her voice carries an air of finality, but I am not onboard with her decree.

"With all due respect, I'm an adult, and I don't need your permission to date somebody." I try to keep any sass from my tone, but I must be unsuccessful because now she looks angry.

"If you're such an adult, you shouldn't be living with your parents anymore. My house, my rules. If you don't like that, you can leave."

Is she serious or is she bluffing? I find it hard to believe that she means what she's saying. She's willing to kick me out over me dating someone she doesn't like?

I take a moment to think about it. I don't know if Josué and I are meant to be, but I also don't see a Biblical reason for me to stop seeing him. And my manman is behaving out of unforgiveness and bitterness. Even if Josué and I aren't meant to be anything more than friendly colleagues, I don't want to validate my manman's thought process by giving in. Which only leaves me with one option.

"I guess I'm leaving then. Am I allowed to pack a few things, or do you want me out right away?" I can tell that I've surprised her. Aha! She was bluffing.

"You can grab a few things."

"Okay, thanks. I'll be out of here soon."

The whole time I'm walking to my room, grabbing a few outfits and packing my toiletries, I expect Manman to take it back and let me stay.

But she does no such thing.

Unsure of whether I should say goodbye, I opt for just leaving silently.

Thankful that the car is mine, I throw my stuff in the backseat and type in Ruthia's address on Google maps. Then, I think of another place I can go to instead.

When I arrive at the condo, I pull into a visitor's parking spot. As I approach the entrance, the doorman waves me in. I head up to the ninth floor and knock on the door in front of the elevator.

"Surprise!" I say when Rarity opens the door.

"Gaelle! Get in here!" she exclaims.

I walk inside the apartment right into a big hug. I forgot she gives the best hugs.

"To what do I owe the pleasure?" she asks as she leads me into the living room.

"Well, I was hoping you had room to take in a stray again?" I ask, gesturing to the duffel bag on my shoulder.

"You're always welcome. Although, I have to ask: are you pregnant?"

At this, I laugh. "Nope, just dating the wrong guy, apparently."

"This sounds like a story I need to hear. I'll heat some water for tea. Feel free to put your things in the guest room."

"Thanks, Rare."

"No worries. We'll chat in a few." I make a right into the familiar hallway that leads to the bedrooms. On my right is the guest room that used to be Ruthia's home before she got married. I spent so much time here with her. I can't believe I'm actually here now for my own reasons; it's a total shock.

I drop my bag on the floor and head to the kitchen where Rarity is at the breakfast bar with two steaming mugs of tea.

"Just in time for your tea. Peppermint is your go-to if I'm remembering correctly." She offers me a mug.

"You're right. Thank you." I take it from her. "Where's Cynthia?"

"She's with my brother for the afternoon. So, your timing is great. We have all the time to spill the tea. Would you prefer divulging your deepest secrets in the living room or here in the kitchen?"

I can't help but laugh. "Let's go to the living room."

We head there together, and each take a corner of her three-seater.

"So, what brings you to my home on this Sunday

afternoon?"

I sigh and explain that I reconnected with my ex and my mom's displeasure with my decision.

"So, he didn't post the pictures?"

"That's right."

"And you guys now have the same faith."

"Yep."

"The same faith as your mom?"

I nod.

"She doesn't believe that he could change. That's the key problem?"

"It seems so."

"No offense, but that's crazy to me. I'm not even a Christian, but I can attest to the way your faith changes people's lives. I saw it in my brother when he became a Christian."

"You did?" I don't bother trying to hide my surprise.

"Oh yeah. He went from being so angry to so gentle. And the way he treated women changed too. He's such a gentleman now. I don't doubt that your God could change Josu - how do I pronounce your boo's name?"

"Josué." I say it slowly for her and she nods.

"Yeah, that. Your God could definitely change his heart, which means He can change your mom's heart too."

Her confidence in God, when she doesn't even fully believe in Him, is both challenging and encouraging to me.

"Thanks, Rare. I needed that reminder."

"No worries."

It hits me we're having a spiritual conversation,

and I can check in on where she's at in this part of her life.

"Rare, I'm curious. How would you describe how you're doing spiritually right now?"

"I'm feeling confident in my belief in God and all, but Jesus is a little intimidating from what I've been reading with Ruthia."

Intimidating? That's the first time I've heard someone describe him that way.

"Can you share more about that?"

"Well sure. If what he said is true, then he's God, and that makes God a lot more..." She struggles to find the word.

"Personal?"

"Yes!" She flashes me a relieved smile. "I just don't know if I can handle that. Jesus has made it clear that He wants our whole lives. Can I give my life?"

I try to temper my excitement. She's so close that she's counting the cost! "That's true but also think about what he offers. Eternal life - a perfect eternity. And abundant life now in the greatest relationship you could ever have. It's like if someone offered you a billion dollars, would you refuse it?"

"When you put it that way, it's, like, no. I wouldn't. What you're describing sounds great..." her voice trails off.

Instinctively, I want to back off. I don't want to pressure her. But I feel the Spirit prompting me to press in, that Rarity can handle it.

"Rare. What do you think is preventing you from accepting Jesus as your Lord and Saviour? Do you feel unworthy? Do you feel you want to play those roles instead?"

She nods. "Yeah, like I want to be my lord and my saviour. I don't want anyone else to be those things for me. After what happened with my ex-husband, I needed to just trust myself."

"And how's that going for you?"

"I love my daughter and my vocation. But I wonder if the emptiness I sometimes feel is normal. Like, is there more to this?"

"It sounds like you being your own lord and saviour has given you a good life, but not a satisfying one?"

"Yes, that's a great way of putting it."

"Well, I can say that there is more to life and that I've never regretted giving those two roles in my life to Jesus. He is fully satisfying and worth surrendering to. But I don't want you to just take my word for it. If you choose to let Him occupy those roles, it has to be because you believe He is better. Better than anyone, including yourself."Tthe words flow out of me and then there's just silence. I almost backtrack, but then she speaks.

"You know, as we've been talking. It feels like my heart has been on fire. In a good way. I think I want to give Jesus a chance to show me He's better. How do I do that?"

I am shook. "Rarity, are you saying that you want to try becoming a Christian?"

She nods. "Yes, can you help me?"

"I can, but I know someone who would love to be part of this moment. Do you mind if I call Ruthia?"

"Not at all."

I take out my phone and swipe to her number. "Hey soeur, what's up? How did today go at church?"

Today at church? Oh yeah! My talk. It feels like that happened ages ago. "It went well. I'm with Rarity. Let me put you on speaker."

"Hey Rare, what's going on?"

"Well, I've decided that I want to become a Christian and Gaelle thought you'd want to be present for this."

Ruthia shrieks, and I almost drop the phone, making Rarity laugh. "Omg! Do you mind if we call Rick? He'd want to be here too."

Rarity gives me an amused look. "Sure, the more the merrier, I guess."

"Great, be back soon."

Ruthia puts us on hold for a moment.

"Ray, is it true? You want to do this?" We hear Roderick say. I can hear the awe in his deep voice.

"Yes, I want to become a Christian. Now, can someone help a girl out and tell me how to do so?"

We all laugh at this. "You just have to talk to God about it." Ruthia tells her.

"Are there any special words I need to say?"

"Not really. You'll want to acknowledge your sin, express your choice to believe that because of what Jesus has done, your sin is covered, and tell Him you want Him to be the Lord and Saviour of your life." I answer her.

"Okay. Here goes it." Rarity closes her eyes and bows her head. "Dear God, I acknowledge that I'm sinful. I've done and thought things that are wrong. Jesus, thank You for Your amazing life and for dying on the cross in my place. I am tired of being my own Lord and Saviour and want to invite You to be that in my life instead. Amen."

"Welcome to the family, sis!" Roderick says excitedly.

"Not me crying through the phone." Ruthia jokes, and we laugh.

"How are you feeling, Rarity?" I ask her.

"I feel fantastic. Like, the emptiness I've been feeling has been filled up." Her voice cracks and I notice that she's beginning to tear up.

I never thought I'd say this, but I'm glad that my manman kicked me out.

Chapter 24

It's been almost a week since I was last in my home, and I'm a verifiable mess of emotions. On one hand, it's been amazing to be with Rarity and her passion for her newfound faith. Every day, we're having conversations about following Jesus and it's so life-giving. But I have this growing tension in my body at Manman and me being in this conflict. Sleep is evading me, and I just don't feel any peace. I could end this by choosing to no longer see Josué, but I don't have peace about that either. Instead, I've just backed off talking to him, telling him I need a bit of space, but I'm still open to a second date.

Our Hawt Messies call today is so needed.

When I see all the ladies' beautiful faces on the screen, I nearly burst into tears. They are my community and I now feel safe enough to fall apart.

Still, as everyone shares how they're doing physically, emotionally, and spiritually, I try to keep it together until Amy calls me out.

"Gaelle, you've been super quiet today. Do you want to share, friend?"

"I mean, my life feels like it's in shambles right now. I'm no longer living at home because I'm in conflict with my manman about dating Josué. I miss home. I miss closeness with Manman, but I think she's wrong about Josué ,and I don't want to stop seeing him. Although, I haven't been talking to him that much because of how conflicted I feel. I'm just all over the place, I guess, and didn't want to monopolize our time with all my problems." It all comes out with a cracked voice as I cry.

"Oh, Gae! It sounds like you're feeling so heavy."

I nod at Michelle's words. That is how I feel.

"I'm so sad for you, love. I was looking forward to getting an update on Josué and your relationship, but now it seems like something that has been a wonderful gift to you has become tainted by this conflict."

Cass is right. This has tinged all the beauty and joy I was experiencing from my connection with Josué, and it sucks.

"Sometimes, our relationships with our parents can be so tricky. I know my mom was my everything for so long that when I saw her sin, it was so disorienting. It catapulted me a bit. Do you feel like that may be what you're experiencing?" Eleora asks.

I find my voice. "Yes. I'm so used to Manman and me being so close and on the same page. I've seen her as a victim of other people's sin, like my father, but I don't think I've ever seen her this way before. Being the one who's hurting me versus comforting me from the hurt."

A chorus of sympathetic sounds ensue from the women.

"How have you and God been since all of this went down?" Hope asks.

"That's a good question. When I'm talking with

Rarity, I'm kind of on autopilot repeating truths about God that new believers need to know, but God and I are not talking right now. I think I've been avoiding Him, to be honest. I might even be angry with Him. Like, why did He have things go this way? Why wouldn't He change my mother's heart to be open towards Josué?"

"Those are valid questions. Maybe it's worth it to ask Him those questions and see what He says." Ruthia comments.

"I know I should, but I think I'm afraid that I won't like the answer. So, I haven't asked." I admit.

"It's been interesting because I've been reading through Ezekiel, which is all about the idolatry of God's people, how He sees it and the consequences of it. It has made me examine myself to see what idols I have in my life. I'm wondering if we may have stumbled across an idol in this situation?"

I consider Hope's gentle but challenging words.

"This may be a dumb question. But what is idolatry? Is that, like, worshipping statues?" Eleora asks.

"Not a dumb question, Ellie." Ruthia says.

"Here, let me pull up a definition by the late Tim Keller that I found helpful in my study." Hope says. We give her a moment and then she reads from her phone. "What is an idol? It is anything more important to you than God, anything that absorbs your heart and imagination more than God, anything you seek to give you what only God can give … An idol is whatever you look at and say, in your heart of hearts, 'If I have that, then I'll feel my life has meaning, then I'll know I have value, then I'll feel significant and secure.' There are many ways to describe that kind of relationship to something, but perhaps the best one is worship."

"Damn, Keller never misses!" Cass says.

"Except for infant baptism, maybe." Michelle jokes and we all laugh. "But seriously, can you share your screen so that we can all see the quote? I feel like there are so many parts to it that are worth sitting in."

"Will do, give just a moment." Hope agrees. After what only feels like a few seconds, we see the quote on the screen. "What parts stand out to you?" She asks us.

"I think for me, it's the part about your imagination. Sometimes, I'm just so captivated by Daniel that he's all that I can think about. I know that's pretty normal when you're in a relationship, but I think it might be subtle idolatry. Like, God is the one who's worth most of my imagination," Cass shares.

"That's a great reminder to us that are dating to not make our relationships an idol, thanks Cass." Eleora comments. "I think I've been an idol before. When Chad was dating me, when I was an unbeliever, he made me more important than God's Word."

"Ooh. That's a great way of knowing if something has been made more important than God to us, if we ignore or disobey God's Word to have it. That'll preach!" Michelle chimes in, making us laugh.

"I think I've made a certain version of motherhood an idol." Ruthia shares after a moment of silence.

"What do you mean?" I ask her, surprised by her admonition.

"Like, I think I have this picture of what it would mean to be the perfect mother. Never using screen time, being at home with them instead of working, able to creatively come up with games and stuff for them to do, and it's like, this pressure that has been on me, and it stirs up so much anxiety because I know that's not me. I think it is an idol because of the last part of the quote. I think I believe that if I could be the perfect mother - according to my own standards - then I would feel significant and that my life is meaningful. I would feel so much better about myself. But the problem is, God is supposed to be where I look to for significance and meaning. God defines me, not how I am as a mother."

"That's powerful, Ruthia. From one mom to another, I resonated with what you just shared. I've been asking God to show me my idols, and He may have just used you to highlight one." Hope shares.

Amy jumps in after her. "I'm enjoying this discussion. I think a past idol of mine was ministry, or the things I was doing for God. I used to look to it for purpose and meaning instead of God. Now that I'm in the workforce, I think I have to be careful to not let my job become that for me. I need to remind myself that what I do doesn't give me value, but the cross gives me value."

I realize that I'm the only one who hasn't yet shared. "I'm not sure what the idol would be in this situation, my relationship with Josué or my relationship with my manman."

"Well, let's line them up against God to see if that helps. If God told you to end your relationship with Josué, would you?" Ruthia asks me.

I don't even have to think about it. "Yes. It would suck, but I would obey Him. I know that, 100%."

"Okay, now let's look at your relationship with your mom. If God told you to do something, but your mom said something different, who would you listen to?"

I know what the right answer should be, but I hesitate on it.

"That slowness to answer might mean that we've stumbled across an idol." Amy comments.

"Let's make it less theoretical. You felt God's call to join staff with Students for Jesus. What if your mom had been against it? Do you think you still would've joined staff?"

I consider Ruthia's words. "I don't know." I admit.

"It sounds to me you need your mother's approval on something to move forward with a decision, maybe more than God's approval?" Cass says gently.

I nod my head, too choked up to speak. I never realized that I had her up on this pedestal, that it felt like I need her say-so just as much or more than God. It's awful to see this in myself.

"How are you feeling with this realization?" Michelle asks.

"I feel gutted. Like, God must be so angry with me for equating Manman with Him." I share.

"Nope, none of that. All of God's anger was put on Jesus, who you've believed in. He doesn't have any anger left over for you, Gaelle, only love," Hope says firmly.

"I think this is just evidence of God's love for you that he let this come out. Earlier, you shared that you've been wondering why God was letting this all happen. It seems to be that a part of the answer may be that He wanted to make you aware of this sin in your life so that you can repent and be holy." Eleora shares.

I nod my head. "How do I repent from this? Like I know I can ask God for forgiveness, but what would it look like for me to turn away from this idolatry?"

"I think your relationship with Josué is one way you can do that. Maybe seek to discern if God wants you two together. If He does, stay with him even if your mom doesn't change her mind. If He doesn't, don't. But when you talk to your mom, maybe emphasize you made the decision because you were following God, not her." Michelle suggests.

I turn her words over in my head. "That sounds like a good plan. But how do I discern this?"

"Well, Shane and I went through a set of questions when we were discerning if God wanted us to get married. I can ask him for them and send them to you?"

"That would be great, Ruthia. Thanks."

"No problem. This has been a great call, guys, but I've gotta get going. Does anyone want to wrap us up in prayer before we all leave?"

"I can pray." Hope volunteers.

I bow my head. "Lord God, thank You for this time for us to meet together today. Thank You, Holy Spirit, for speaking during this time. For surfacing idolatry in our lives and giving us a space to be accountable to each other. I pray You would help us all to repent of idolatry and worship You alone as our God. I pray specifically for Gaelle, that you would help her discern whether she and Josué should be together. We know You have a good plan, and we ask that You would reveal that to her. In Jesus's name, amen."

"Amen." I whisper, wiping away a few tears.

"Alrighty ladies, we'll have our next call in a month. Talk to you later!" Ruthia says with a wave. We all wave to each other on the screen and then leave the call.

I'm so thankful for this time.

Chapter 25

Josué told me to leave the whole day open for this date, so, with only a teensy bit of trepidation, I cleared my schedule. I'm waiting outside Rarity's building, expecting to see Josué on foot, so I'm surprised when he rolls up in a black SUV.

"New car?" I ask him as I hop into the passenger seat.

"Rental." He responds and then turns off the car. I look at him in surprise. "Gaelle, I have to say that I'm very confused. You said that you wanted to come on this date but that you also need space from me and so we haven't talked. I do not know where your head is at right now, and it's throwing me into a tailspin."

"I'm sorry that this has been confusing. My manman and I had a huge fight about me seeing you that culminated in me being kicked out of my home." His mouth opens in shock. "I didn't want to tell you this and hurt you, but I also haven't known what to do since, so I asked for that space. Where I'm at now is that I know I like you a lot and want to see where this goes."

He looks like he doesn't know what to say to all that I've shared. "I'm feeling conflicted things. On the one hand, I am so happy that you feel the same way about me as I feel about you. But you and your manman are so close, I hate that I've come between you two. I don't know if a relationship with me is worth all this trouble that it's caused."

I take his left hand in my right one. "Josué, it's not your fault. And it is worth it if it's God's will for us to be together because obeying Him is always worth it."

"I guess that means that we need to figure out what His will is for us, sooner than later."

I nod my head in agreement. "Exactly. Ruthia forwarded me some relationship questions to answer that might help with that discerning. Are you down to go through them with me? I know that's pretty heavy for a second date."

"I mean, I was planning on us having a day at Niagara Falls, so we have a lot of driving time to fill. Why not go through these questions? The worst that can happen is that we see that we're incompatible as romantic partners, but maybe still able to be good friends. And while that's not what I want, it would be easier to know this before you take more of my heart."

His words feel like they're reverberating through my head. "I have some of your heart?"

He looks at me like I just asked him a stupid question. "Yes. It was torture not talking to you for the past week and a half. I missed you, Gae." His voice cracks on my nickname, and he clears his throat, turning away from me.

Deciding to be brave, I lean over the gearshift, reach for his face, and turn his head back towards me. I can feel him slightly lean into my touch, and I'm hit with just how much he must care for me and how honoured I feel to have that be true. It makes it easy to admit something that I've been avoiding for the last nine days. "I missed you too, Josué."

With his free hand, he cradles my face, and we're mirror images, each holding onto the other, our faces only centimetres apart, so close that I feel his exhale on my lips.

"I want to kiss you right now, Gaelle." My heartbeat speeds up at this pronouncement.

"I'm okay with that." I breathe out, ready to close my eyes and receive his kiss.

"But I want to do things differently this time. I want to honour God and you better than I did before."

I'm a mix of disappointment and desire. "You know, that only makes me want to kiss you more."

He laughs and then closes the distance between us, kissing me on the cheek and then pulling back. Feeling dazed, I return to sitting in my seat. Who knew a kiss on the cheek could be so damn hot?

"Maybe we should get to those questions." He suggests, turning the car back on.

"Sure, I must warn you they're pretty deep."

"I'm ready." he says.

"Okay, when do you want to get married? What would you like the timeline to be for how long we are dating and engaged?"

"Bet, okay. I think at least one year of dating and at least 6-9 months of engagement."

"That sounds pretty reasonable to me. I've heard that long engagements are difficult, so the shorter that can be regarding planning, the better. Okay, would you be open to going to therapy, before or after we are married?"

"Oh, for sure. Pre-marital or pre-engagement counselling is a must."

"Facts." I agree. "And for afterwards, I think it might be good to go for counselling every so often for a marital check-up."

"I never thought of that before, but that's wise, Gaelle."

"Thanks. Next up: Is divorce an option?"

"I have to think about this one."

"No worries, I can share first. I think the Bible only gives two allowances for divorce: adultery and if a non-believing spouse wants to end the marriage. Still, I think I would want to try counselling or redemptive separation before bringing up divorce."

"Redemptive separation?"

"Being separated but working towards a healthy and holy marriage. I think I heard John Piper first use the term."

"You've given me a lot to think about. Honestly, divorce is so common in our society that I just assumed that if your marriage isn't working, it can be ended. I didn't know what the Bible had to say about it. But I agree with you. I would rather have a redemptive separation than divorce any day."

"Sweet. Okay, now on the topic of kids. How soon would you like to try for children? How many children do you want, if any? Would you ever adopt?"

I should feel apprehension about asking these big questions, but I feel peace. Like, I want to know his thoughts on these things, and I feel comfortable enough with him that he will not run because of them.

"At least 2 years before kids and at least 2 kids. I'm super down to adopt. It would be such a cool way to display the gospel!"

"I like those answers. I think for kids, I'd just want an even number so no one ever feels left out. You know?"

"I do. What's next?"

I laugh at his eagerness. "You're enjoying this."

"Yeah, it's helping me put words to things I haven't taken a ton of time to think about. And I enjoy learning new things about you."

I smile at how his words mirror my thoughts. "Okay, how would you discipline our children if they misbehave?" I stumble over the word 'our' a bit. That paltry word carries with it such intimacy.

"Hmm. I'm not opposed to spanking, but I also am not gungho about it either. Does that make sense?"

I nod my head. "It does. It's been cool seeing Ruthia be a mom and learning from her. She and Shane are trying to gentle parent, so no spanking or time outs. It focuses more on emotional regulation and parenting for the heart, not just the behaviour. From what I've observed, it's difficult, but it's supposed to be worth it."

"I haven't heard of that before, but it makes sense. Like, changing behaviour is usually accomplished by fear. I want my kid to respect me, but that doesn't mean they have to fear me."

I feel my heart expand in my chest at his words.

"Same. Okay, what type of schooling do you want your children to go to? How do you want them to be educated?"

"As a missionary, I see the opportunity of meeting parents and being in the community by putting my kids in public school. But I'm not sure how I feel about the sex-ed curriculum and the worldview they'd be under.

To be honest, I'm a bit torn."

"Yep. I feel that. I think if our kids," there's that word again carrying a huge weight, but it slips off the tongue easier this time, "were in public school, there'd need to be a lot of proactivity on our part to lay a solid gospel foundation for them."

"Oh, that's a non-negotiable."

The firmness with which he speaks makes my … uterus tingle? It's like I can hear it screaming at me to make babies with this man. "Alright, time for the third huge topic: finances."

"Lay it on me."

It takes all the self-control I possess to not imagine me laying something on him, alright.

"Who would pay for the wedding and how will we deal with that expense?"

"Well, my mom sold her house when we all moved out and gave us each a portion of the profit, so I have enough savings for a wedding, a modest one at least."

I gape at him. "I was not expecting you to say that."

"I'm a man of mystery, Gaelle."

"Clearly. Okay, the next question is: How do you spend your money? Do you consider yourself a saver or a spender? For me, I probably am 55% a saver and 45% a spender. Like, I don't rush to spend money, but I'm okay with spending it when I need to."

"I'm probably 65% a spender, 35% a saver. But that's why I use a spending tracker app on my phone so that I can monitor my budget and adjust myself as needed."

"Ooh. I need that in my life. What's the name of the app?"

"Wilbur."

"As in the pig, like a piggy bank!" My delight over this is clear in my squeal and makes him laugh.

"What's the next question?"

"If someone gave you $5 million, no strings attached—where would you live, what would you do for a career and to who/how much would you give away?"

"Oof. I would love to be here in Brampton, probably in a large home for the kids and for being hospitable. Maybe even having international students live with us."

I feel my face warm at how easily he says 'us'.

"I would want to do the same job but keep my salary low. And I'd give at least a million to missions in the 10/40 window. Probably spread it around between Bible translation, church planting, and compassion projects."

I love his answer so much. Jesus said that our heart is revealed in how we use our treasure, and it's obvious that his heart beats for the kingdom of God. I can feel my feelings for him growing as we go through these questions.

It would be hard to dial back if God said no to us.

"That's a wonderful answer. I can't say that I disagree with any of it. Pay off a large house and a couple of reliable cars, give a chunk away to the causes that you just shared and then maybe invest some of it with a professional? That way, we could get what I think is called passive income, and that allows our salaries to stay low."

"These questions are showing me just how wise you are, Gaelle. I hadn't even thought of that last part, but I'm down for it."

I smile at him and then glance down at my phone for the next question. "Okay, our next taboo topic for a second date is sex."

I feel the car swerve and look at him in surprise.

"Are you okay?"

"Yeah, just not what I was expecting you to say." He answers quickly.

"Okay, do you still want to work through these questions?"

"Let's do this." He sounds resolute.

"Alright, what are your beliefs about pornography? If you struggle with this, how are we going to work on overcoming it?" Yikes, this question is personal.

"Well, that was one thing that changed about my life when I came to Christ. The way some people can leave smoking or drinking miraculously happened for me with pornography. I know it can be a long-term struggle for many people, and my story is uncommon, but that's what happened to me."

"Wow. Thanks for sharing that with me. Okay, when do you believe it is okay to have sex? Are you willing to abstain until marriage?"

"Yes. I believe that's the context that sex is meant to happen within, and I want to honour God and my future wife in this way. Obviously, before knowing Christ I failed in this area. But ever since following Him, I've been committed to abstinence."

"Amen." I affirm him. "Alright, last one. What do you consider infidelity? Hmm. For me, this goes beyond a sexual act. I think emotional cheating would hurt me more."

"True. I didn't even think of that, but it would be

hurtful if my wife was romantically bonding with someone else."

I nod my head emphatically. "I like the way you worded that. 'Romantically bonding'. Okay, that's the last of the questions."

"Really?"

"Well, there are some more, but we've already talked through them, so they feel non-essential."

"Fair enough. How are you feeling about it all?"

"I feel…" my voice trails off as I try to figure out what's going on inside of me. "I think I feel peace? Like, all I see from our answers to these questions are green flags. That we would be good together long term. What about you?"

To my surprise, he crosses over three lanes on the highway to take the next exit. I look up and we are still a ways from Niagara Falls. He pulls into a gas station right by the highway exit and then turns off the car. Then, he turns towards me. I forget to breathe for a second when I see the look on his face. It's ablaze with a gravity that I've yet to see on his face before.

"I'm even more sure now that you're wifey material, Gaelle. It was not hard to paint a picture of the future with us together, and I have no doubt in my mind that it would be good." His words bring a feeling of rightness to me, like a feeling of coming home.

"I was going to save this for later in the day, but I'd like to ask you to be my girlfriend, Gaelle. I want us to be dating, meaning that we're discerning whether we should one day get married. I once told you that you're it for me. I was young and foolish then, but even a broken clock is right twice a day. And I believe I got that part right. I haven't been with anyone since you, save for a few dates here and there, and I am sure that I am on my way to falling back in love with you, if I ever stopped loving you in the first place. And I'm not sure that I did."

This is one of the most important moments of my life. A man of God all but declaring his love for me and my entire being longing to reciprocate that love. Feeling like God has given His blessing on it. But feeling is not the same as knowing, and I want to know. There's still my manman to be dealt with. Is Josué God's will for my life as a husband? As I struggle to find the right words to say, he speaks again.

"Gaelle, I don't want you to feel pressured to reciprocate my feelings. I didn't share them with you so that I could hear them back. I said all that I did because I want you to have no doubts regarding how I see you and feel about you. I understand if you need some time before you respond. I already know that you care about me, and that's enough right now."

I begin to tear up. This kind, wonderful, patient man has just let me off the hook, and it makes me love him all that much more. There, I can admit it - at least to myself. I'm falling in love with him again.

He leans over and wipes away my tears.

"Thank you."

"You're welcome." The smile that he's giving me is so earnest that it makes my heart ache. If only Manman hadn't given such a disapproval, adding so much pressure to me discerning rightly about us being together. If she took the time to know him, she wouldn't disapprove. Then an idea occurs to me.

"Josué, would you be willing to meet with my manman and I and give her a chance to know the new you?" Even I can hear the nerves in my voice.

"That's an easy yes, Gaelle. Just let me know when and I'll clear my calendar."

"Will do." I feel good about this. It'll work.

It has to.

Chapter 26

"**Where does this** leave us, Gaelle?" Josué asks me as we pull into the parking lot of his apartment building. We've been silent the entire car ride from the restaurant.

"I'm not sure." I try to hold back my tears as I let my head fall on the steering wheel. Tonight did not go the way I wanted it to at all.

I was so sure it would go well. When my manman's text agreeing to meet with us had come in right after an encouraging support appointment, I was sure that it was all going to work out. That I could trust Him with this situation, the same way I trust Him in support raising.

I was wrong.

"My feelings for you are unchanged." The firmness of his voice feels steadying, like something that can cut through my confusion. "Do you still feel the same way about me?"

I look up at the vulnerability that I hear in his voice. I long to assure him. "Yes, I do." He relaxes. "I just don't think that my feelings for you are enough for me to make this decision to be in a relationship with you. I need to sort out God's will in this situation."

"That's what dating is for." He points out.

"True, but this is an extenuating circumstance. I feel like I need to know that dating you is what God wants before we start out so that I can justify going against my manman like this."

"I can understand that, but I don't like it."

I sigh. "Me neither."

"I'm guessing you're going to want some space again?"

I hadn't even thought of that. This past week since our date, we've been texting throughout our days and talking on the phone together at night. If I'm going to discern this, though, he might be right.

"I don't want it, but I think I'll need it."

"Okay, I guess I'll see you at new staff training in a few days."

That feels way too far away, but I nod in agreement.

"Bye for now, Gaelle." His voice was sad.

"Bye Josué." He leaves the car and my chest pains in protest. Is a part of my heart breaking already? Just at being distant from him?

I wipe away a few escaped tears and then resolve to hold it together until I get to Rarity's.

I'll let myself fall apart there.

I drive and park on autopilot. As I take out my key fob for the building, I feel wetness on my face. I hoped that I could return these tonight. I had packed my bag with such hope that I would go back home.

I'm so glad I have this moment of private weeping. When I get to the apartment's front door, I don't even have to use my key. It opens up for me.

Ruthia's smile falls into a look of concern for me.

"Oh, soeur…" Her voice trails off, and she opens her arms wide. I step into them.

Now, in the arms of my best friend, I can fall apart.

I sob, and she holds me even tighter. I'm not sure how long we stay like that in the front hallway, but when my sobs subside, she pulls back to look at my face and then wipes away my last remaining tears with her thumb.

"You are dearly loved, soeur. No matter what happened tonight, I need you to know that."

I nod my head. "Merci."

"Shall we go to the living room and talk about it all?"

Again, I give her a head nod, and she takes my arm and leads me to the couch, sitting beside me. Soon, a mug of tea is being offered to me. I look up to see Rarity giving me a gentle smile.

"Do you want me to make myself scarce for this conversation?" she asks.

"No, you can stay. I need all the love I can get." She sits beside Ruthia and then they're both looking at me.

"So, what happened tonight? How did it start?"

"We were waiting at the restaurant. When she came to our table, Josué stood up to shake her hand, and she just stared at it."

"Yikes." Ruthia comments.

"And if you'll believe it, it only gets worse from there. She didn't even check in on how I've been or greet me. She just sat down and immediately started asking Josué questions."

"Like, what?" Rarity asks.

"Oh, everything from his testimony to his church

involvement to employment to politics. It was a straight up interrogation."

"What did you think of Josué's answers?"

I take a moment to think about Ruthia's question. "I liked all of them. Some I already knew, and others were a pleasant surprise. I lean more left than my parents, and it was cool to see that Josué leans left too but has such a robust Biblical backing for it. He's thought it through a lot more than I have."

"Now, I'm curious, but it's not about my curiosity but your processing. Your mom didn't like any of his answers?"

"No, I don't think she did. Often, she would just dismiss his answer. Like, for example, she was really judgy about his testimony."

"I don't understand."

"Neither do I, Rare. What's more, she was unhappy about him being in ministry. She doesn't think that he'd be able to provide for me if we were to get married."

"But you're also in ministry." Ruthia points out.

"I know. It makes no sense to me. Like, I think this is a viewpoint on gender that is maybe different for her? I don't know."

"I can hear how frustrated you are. Did anything else happen?" Ruthia asks.

"She brought up our past and how heartbroken I was when everything went down. She said that she didn't want me to come to her crying when it goes badly like last time because she would just want to tell me she told me so."

"That's cold." Ruthia begins to rub circles on my back, and I lean into her comforting touch.

"Sorry, remind me, your mom is a believer in Jesus?" Rarity confirms.

"Yep."

"This makes less and less sense. Josué isn't just some random guy then, he's her brother in Christ. It doesn't sound like she's treating him like that, just finding every opportunity to tear him down."

"Yes, exactly."

"How is he doing after all of this?"

Rarity's question shouldn't catch me off guard, but it does. "He still feels the same way about me, but I didn't even ask how he was actually feeling in general. I imagine he would feel angry or hurt. That's how I felt on his behalf, at least."

"Makes sense. So, what happens now?"

"Well, Josué and I are going to give each other some space while I discern whether I should be his girlfriend." I can't keep the sadness out of my voice.

"I hate how much pressure this has put on you. Like, dating is already a discerning process that has weight on it. But now you have this added part, too."

"Exactly! This pressure makes me just want to run from the situation, but I can't. I have to deal with it. I have to figure out what God has to say about all of this."

"Well, how has God spoken to you regarding decision making in the past?" Rarity asks.

The question shouldn't be so difficult to answer.

"Well, if it's not a matter of sin, I talk things over with my manman and Ruthia. It always just felt like if my manman was good with it, God was to."

I'm hit again with how much I've elevated my mother's will throughout my life instead of God's will.

"It sounds like you're going to need a fresh encounter with God, Gaelle. You can't rely on your mom anymore."

I sigh and lean my head against Ruthia's shoulder as her words really hit me. I should be excited to experience God in a new way, but I'm more scared and resigned. I was comfortable with how I decided things. "I know."

"Well, we'll be praying for you. It won't do you good to hear our opinions on this. You need to hear from God yourself. And I'm sure that He will speak." Rarity's confidence in God both chastises and inspires me.

"And in the meantime, we're here for you." Ruthia adds and wraps an arm around me, giving me a brief side hug.

I smile at them with teary eyes, not expecting that on a night so terrible I could still feel so loved and safe. It didn't go the way I wanted, but there's still goodness even now, right here with my sisters.

Chapter 27

I wish I could miss today's training. I haven't even done the prep work. I'm not in the mood to see Josué after what happened on Sunday. I'm not in a condition to be interacting with people right now, even virtually. I just want to go back to what I've been doing for the last few days: crying in bed and watching Glee.

With a sigh, I sign onto the call and am the last one to join. Victoria smiles at the screen. "Welcome Gaelle. Okay guys, we're going to dive right into our topic today: Listening to God and Discerning His Will."

I don't know whether to laugh or cry.

It's a good training. We talk about His will being our sanctification, barriers to obeying His will, and how to determine the seriousness of a matter that we're trying to discern. What stands out to me the most is when Victoria talks about people-pleasing.

"Some of us, and I include myself here, are people-pleasers. We live to do what others want to the point of deep fear, pressure, or even anxiety when others are upset with us. Sometimes, following God's will overlaps with what others want us to do, but often it doesn't and then we need to make a choice: God or people?"

I can barely pay attention to the rest of the training, because I'm so focused on these words. Once it's done, I push aside my laptop and stare up at the ceiling.

"Okay God, You got my attention. You want me to talk to You. You *want* me to know Your will in this situation." I sigh. "I'm sorry for avoiding You these past few days. Whatever answer You give me will come with some kind of pain, and I don't want to experience it - whether it's losing a relationship with Josué or losing one with my manman."

It would suck to not date and maybe even marry him one day, but losing my manman is something that I cannot fathom. Then again, the thought of Josué being with someone else leaves an empty gnawing in my chest.

I feel the all too familiar tingle in my eyes that indicates tears.

"Okay God. I'm tired of living in the limbo of not knowing what Your will is. I want what You want for me, no matter what it is."

"Remember."

His voice is so loud that it feels like it was almost audible. What does He want me to remember? And then, I feel prompted by the Spirit to open my journal. I retrieve it from my night table and flip backwards until I land on the first day of New Staff Training.

Oh.

God told me He would refine me that day. I thought He was referring to the process of support raising and then maybe reconciling with Josué, but could He have meant more than that? Could dating Josué be how He wants to refine me out of the idolatry of people-pleasing?

"Lord, am I on the right track? Is this what you're saying to me? Do you really want me to go against my manman like this?"

I then sense Holy Spirit prompting me to Luke 14. When I get to verse 26, I know why He led me here.

"If anyone comes to Me, and does not hate his own father and mother and wife and children and brothers and sisters, yes, and even his own life, he cannot be My disciple. Whoever does not carry his own cross and come after Me cannot be My disciple. For which one of you, when he wants to build a tower, does not first sit down and calculate the cost to see if he has enough to complete it?"

"Okay, God. You're making Yourself very clear. You want me to follow You even if it means conflict with someone I care about deeply. This is part of the cross You want me to carry and the cost of obeying You in this situation." I sigh.

"Gaelle, I promised you it would be hard, but I also promised an abundance of good."

And then an image comes to mind. It's edged in white and I see myself on the arm of God. He's blurry, like I can't figure out exactly what He looks like, but I know in my soul that it's Him. We're walking together with our arms hooked together. It zooms out and I see where we're walking to - or rather, who we're walking to.

Josué.

The smile he gives me makes me feel paradoxically grounded and like I could take flight at any moment.

God places my hands in his and then moves in between us. "Therefore, what I have joined together, let no one separate."

Immediately, the scene changes. Josué and I have aged a bit and are standing on a dirt road with palm trees around us facing a large light blue house. A little Black girl comes running towards us, her braids flying as she does so. She jumps into my arms, and Josué encircles us both in a group hug.

I'm jolted back to reality and feel like I can finally take a breath. Sure, I've had spiritual dreams before, but God has never given me visions of the future. And I know that's what those were.

A future where Josué and I are together, and we have an … adopted daughter?

I'm filled with an immeasurable joy. So much so that I begin to laugh and cry. My body does not know how to handle what I saw.

"Thank You, Lord, for being kind enough to give me a glimpse of Your plan. It is good. And I submit to it gladly and wholeheartedly. I trust You. Amen."

With those words comes hope and peace to accompany the joy, reminding me of Romans 15:13: 'Now may the God of hope fill you with all joy and peace as you believe so that you may overflow with hope by the power of the Holy Spirit.'

I was dreading whatever future God had in store for me, forgetting that He is good and He works all things for good. Now, I feel a keen hope even though I know there will be hardship.

I'm not sure who I should tell about God's revelation first, Ruthia, Josué or Manman.

I think about it for a moment and then I pick up my phone to call Manman. Better to get the hardest conversation out of the way.

This is the first time I've called her since she kicked me out. It rings for so long that I think it's going to go to voicemail, but at the last moment I hear a click.

"Bonswa, Gaelle."

"Bonswa, Manman."

"I'm glad that you've come to your senses. When will you be home?"

I must've missed something. "Pardon?"

"You're calling to say that you realized I was right and that you want to come home now, right?"

Wrong. So wrong. "Not exactly. I'm calling to let you know I intend to date Josué and marry him one day."

Silence.

"But you don't have my blessing." She sounds confused.

"I know, and that hurts, but I feel I have God's blessing."

"Do you think that I'm not hearing from God? You don't trust God in me?"

Oh boy, that's a tough question to answer. "I believe you know and love God. I also believe that your judgement may be clouded by what happened in the past."

"How dare you say that?"

"I don't mean to be disrespectful, ,Manman, I was just trying to honestly answer your question."

"So, you're really going to go forward without my blessing?" Her repeated questioning almost makes me doubt my resolve, but then I remember the visions that God gave me and the refining process He's invited me into.

"Yes, I really am. Mwen renmen ou *[I love you]*,

Manman. That has not changed. But I need to obey God."

"How do you know that you're not just doing what you want and saying that it's God who's leading you?"

I sigh. "Because I wouldn't want to jeopardize our relationship like this, no matter the guy. This is the harder path, Manman."

"I see. Well, I disagree with you, and I will not give you my blessing, but I still want you to come back home. I've missed you. I'm not ready to be an empty nester just yet."

Her words are both cutting and comforting. I've missed her too. I've missed home. "I can be home by tonight."

"Sa se bèl bagay *[that's wonderful]*. See you soon."

"N a we [*See you later*]!"

I hear her hangup the phone and stare at it in awe. That could've gone better, but it also could've gone a lot worse. The fact that our relationship isn't completely ruined by my decision is God's kindness and power in action.

"Thank you, thank you, thank you Lord." I whisper.

Buoyed by that call, I decide to text Josué and be a little cheeky while I'm at it.

I've had enough space.

It's not long before a reply comes in.

Is that your way of saying that you miss me?

I laugh a bit at this. I'm still thinking of what to say when another text comes in.

Because I miss you.

My heart flutters.

Do you have any free time to meet today? We need to talk.

Instantly, he replies.

Sure. I'm at the downtown library, so I'm near to you. Meet at city hall?

That's sooner than I expected, but not unwanted. I could make it there in fifteen but want to sneak in a shower. In my moping, I had neglected my personal hygiene.

Sounds good. See ya in half an hour?

He reacts with a thumb up to my message, and I put down my phone. Now, what does one wear to tell a guy that she's discerned that God wants them together?

I turn over different outfit combinations in my head while I head to the shower. By the time I'm out, I decide on a flowy light yellow sundress and let my faux locs go loose instead of pulled back in my usual braid or ponytail.

I feel free, and I want to look like that too.

It's a short walk to city hall from Rarity's, made beautiful by the only slightly cloudy blue sky and gentle breeze that moves my hair around my shoulders.

I see him right away sitting on a wall.

I still don't understand how it's possible to make shorts and a t-shirt look so good. They just fit him so well, showcasing his strong and solid body. It's crazy to me that God would choose this gorgeous man to be mine.

But He has.

And knowing this so assuredly in the core of who I am and who God has called me to be brings me so much joy that I can't stop the smile that lights my face.

He must feel my eyes on him because he turns in

my direction, and I'm struck by how tortured he looks. Is he okay?

"It's giving cruelty, Gaelle."

Cruel? What could he mean? "I don't understand."

"If you're going to break my heart, I can accept that. But to delay it and execute it while looking like sunshine embodied… that doesn't seem cruel to you?"

It takes a moment for his words to register. "What makes you think that I'm going to break your heart?"

"You said that we need to talk." He points out, and I blanch. That may not have been the best word choice I've ever made.

"I'm sorry for misleading you. That's not what I meant at all." I say firmly, and he goes from tortured to curious, maybe even hopeful. I choose to sit down beside him, extremely aware of the chasm of an inch that separates us.

"What did you want to talk about, then?" He asks after a moment.

I fiddle with my hands in my lap. Why didn't I practice what I was going to say?

"Well, us. I've been doing some praying and seeking of the Lord for His will for us having a future together." I pause here, not knowing exactly what to say next. I don't want to be that girl that is all 'God told me you're going to be my husband' even if that's true.

"And…?"

I take a deep breath. Why does this feel so scary? "I believe God wants us to be together, that He sees us being in a relationship as a good thing."

I look up to see his reaction.

His joy is evident and makes me release the breath that I hadn't even realized I'd been holding.

"You have no idea how glad I am to hear you say that. Ever since I read your text, I was sure that you were going to say the opposite and was wrestling with God on how to let you go when it feels like He's been imprinting you upon my heart. I love you, Gaelle."

What does me in is the way he declares his love for me so gingerly, as if he's nervous that it's unreciprocated; as if he's taking a risk in saying those three words.

I never want him to be nervous around me again. I want him to be so sure of my love for him that it never feels like a risk to love me because he knows I feel the same way. It's with great delight that I confidently stare into his eyes and say, "I love you too, Josué."

To my surprise, I see tears form in his eyes. He closes them for a moment and when he opens them again, I see a single tear descending from each one.

I lean towards him and raise my hand to wipe them away, but he gently stops me, taking that same hand in his own. With his other hand, he runs a hand through my hair before placing it on the back of my neck. Tenderly, he nudges me closer toward him so that our foreheads are touching each other. I feel his every inhale and exhale as we breathe in tandem.

My eyes must express my desire for him as his lighten with desire right before he closes the distance between us and seals our hearts' declarations with a kiss.

Dear Reader,

I hope you came to enjoy Gaelle and Josué's story!

With this novel, I hoped to showcase what it's like to be a vocational missionary in a local setting, in regards to the support raising process and the training that they experience. I once held this role and I have people I love who still do, including my husband. I have yet to read about their experiences in the Christian romance space, so it was important for me to do that here.

Another real experience that is not often written in the Christian romance space is parental disapproval for non-Biblical reasons. I wanted to highlight how difficult that can be and what it looks like to trust and obey God even in that situation. May we all find courage to not please people, but please God, wherever we find ourselves.

"Therefore, my dear brothers and sisters, be steadfast, immovable, always excelling in the Lord's work, because you know that your labor in the Lord is not in vain." - 1 Corinthians 15:58 CSB

Grace and peace,
    Sana'